I0727141

Curse:
Rose Red Retold

DEMELZA CARLTON

A tale in the Romance a Medieval Fairy Tale series

DEDICATION

This one is for Lana, who reminded me that expanding
universes are a good thing.

.

One

When Boris laid down his sword at the end of the day, it felt so much heavier than when he'd buckled it on this morning. Was it the weight of the lives he'd taken, or the blood the blade had drunk during battle?

"I brought water for you to wash, Your Highness," Igor said, sloshing the contents of his bucket into the bowl before the squire dropped the bucket on the floor. "Do you want me to help you out of your armour, too?"

Boris was perfectly capable of taking his own clothes off, and any other day he'd have said so, but they'd been fighting since dawn, and there wasn't a bit of his body that wasn't complaining of weariness. "Please," he said instead, lifting his aching arms to give the boy better access to the buckles on his breastplate.

His previous squire wouldn't have asked — he'd have simply made himself useful, but Kyrilu had earned his knighthood a year ago now, and he now served Boris's brother, Yarik, in the north. Igor still had some growing to do, as well as a lot of learning, before he'd be as good as Kyrilu.

"It'll need a good clean and polish before the morrow, for we march for home in the morning," Boris added.

Igor's thin shoulders lifted in a massive sigh. "Yes, Your Highness." He'd learned not to complain, but his sulky expression said he wanted to.

Boris hid his smile. He hadn't liked cleaning armour at Igor's age, either, but he'd known blood could eat at steel like rust, weakening what needed to be strong. Armour had saved his life more than once, and Boris appreciated the value of well-maintained gear.

"Tell the cook I'm ready for supper, too," Boris said. "After that, I won't need you until breakfast."

Igor nodded and dashed away.

Boris barely had time to finish washing and don fresh clothes before his knights began to arrive to deliver their reports of the day's battle.

"I lost six of my men today in an ambush, but we found the Bisseni camp."

Which wouldn't have had much of value in it. The food they'd stolen from the villages south of here was likely long gone,

"All our dead are buried, Your Highness. Far fewer than the enemy dead. My men are still working on the pit to bury all of them."

Boris wasn't sure the Bisseni would appreciate the good Christian burial his men gave them, but as they were dead, they weren't likely to complain about it.

"We're down two horses, but only minor wounds among the men."

Two warhorses would be costly to replace,

but the knights who'd lost them could surely afford it. As they'd all head home on the morrow, it wasn't likely they'd need new warhorses until next year's campaign.

"My scouts report no more Bisseni within a day's ride."

No Bisseni they could see, anyway. The mountain dwellers could be hiding under a rock just outside camp, and they'd never know until someone decided to use the rock as a latrine.

"Your supper, Your Highness."

Igor was getting better at not spilling the stew. The pot was still more than half full.

"Two of the Bisseni got away, vanished into the mountains."

If only they'd stay in the mountains, instead of coming to raid their villages. Then Boris and his men could stay at home, polishing benches with their ever-broadening butt-cheeks as they feasted on this victory until the next enemy dared to invade their borders.

Boris suppressed a smile. He and his men were not made for polishing benches, or growing fat from feasting. Much like his father, who would have ridden out with them, had his health not prevented it.

"Where to next, Your Highness?"

Boris raised his head to find all his men watching him with an air of expectation. Good men, loyal men, who had earned a victory feast a dozen times over during this gruelling campaign.

"On the morrow, we pack up and head for the capital. God willing, we'll be feasting in Prislav before we know it!"

A ragged cheer rose up, followed by a chorus of thanks. To him, to God, to the saints and whoever else they prayed to in the heat of battle.

"Your father would be proud, Your Highness," said Sir Cyril, the oldest of his knights.

Boris acknowledged the older man's praise with a grave nod. "Indeed. As am I, to have fought with so many good men, in my father's stead."

The men trooped out, leaving Boris with his now empty supper bowl. He couldn't remember eating a bite, he'd been so busy.

Probably for the best — those newly dead warhorses had likely gone into the stewpot.

The court in Prislav might not be his favourite place to be, but at least his father's kitchens served more than old horse.

Even better would be a meal at home, with his wife and daughter. Would baby Lida be walking and talking yet? She'd barely learned to smile before he left. How would she have changed in the months he'd been away? He couldn't wait to find out.

Boris blew out the candle and lay down to dream of family dinners instead of fierce fighters who wanted him dead. He was going home.

Two

"And this is my heart," Mother said, placing Rossa's hand on her breast. Through the layers of linen and wool, Rossa could barely feel the thump of her mother's heart. Not like when her hand was against her own skin.

If she could just reach through the wool and linen…

Rossa bit down so hard on her lip that it hurt. She opened her mouth to cry out, but then she felt it. The deep drum of her mother's heart, as it squeezed and expanded inside her.

Fascinated, she focussed on the heart, and

the blood pumping through it. Streaming out in a thousand directions, keeping her mother alive. She could look, but not touch, the memories from her ancestors told her. To touch was to kill, and an enchantress never used her magic for evil.

"They come! They come!"

The shout from above, followed by thunderous footsteps racing to the bottom of the tower sent Mother's heart fluttering like a bird's wings.

"What is it, Raphael?" Mother asked.

The healer man who lived in the topmost tower room stuck his head through the tapestry into Mother's chamber. His eyes were fever-bright. "I don't know, but there's a large party coming up the road. Maybe they've come to tell us it's safe to go home!"

His head disappeared and Rossa heard his feet on the stairs once more.

Mother said a bad word. "Stay here in the tower, Rossa. I will come fetch you when it's safe."

Rossa nodded.

Mother left.

Rossa grew tired of sitting alone in Mother's chamber, so she pushed the tapestry aside and climbed to the top of the tower, where Raphael kept watch. She wasn't sure what he watched for, but she knew it made him frown and sigh a lot.

But when she reached the top, she couldn't find Raphael, and she was too short to see out the windows.

She repeated Mother's bad word. Several times. But it didn't lift her any higher. She said the bad word again, then headed down the stairs. She'd be able to see the road from the bailey.

It was a long climb for her short legs, but Rossa kept going. She wanted to see the party.

There was no one in the great hall, but someone had left the doors open, as if they knew she was coming. Giggling, she broke into a run. After only a few steps, she tripped on the uneven flagstones and went sprawling.

Pain flared in her shin, and Rossa let out a yowl.

"Rossa?"

That was Mother. Mother would take her to

the stillroom and cover her in smelly herbs and bandages and she'd miss the party. Rossa jumped to her feet and raced for the doors.

"Rossa! Get back here! Rossa!"

Mother could not run as fast as her. This was a race, and Rossa knew she would win.

Daddy was in the bailey, and he always caught her. Rossa ran straight for him. Sure enough, he scooped her up in his arms, sending her soaring like the eagles higher up in the mountains.

But there was a horse coming, heading straight for Daddy. Focussing on the still-stinging graze on her shin, Rossa held up her hand to stop the horse.

The horse rose up on his back legs, almost like he was dancing. The fat man on his back rolled off and landed in the dirt.

Rossa giggled. She'd never seen a man roll like a ball before. Oh, but the horse did not like dancing. Rossa reached out, touching the horse's back, so he set his hooves on the ground again. Only she hadn't reached with her hand, but with an invisible hand made of magic.

The fat man got up and said things to Daddy and Mother. Daddy stiffened, his arm tightening around Rossa while his other hand went for his sword.

Daddy only used his sword on evil men, he'd told her. To cut out their evil hearts. That meant the fat man was evil. Would his heart look different to Mother's?

Rossa reached out, just to look, not to touch. The evil man's heart was different to Mother's. It looked like it was straining, not strong enough to pump the blood, which didn't stream like Mother's. There was a dark lump trapped inside.

Was that what evil looked like?

Mother shouted for a healer, drawing Rossa out of her reverie.

The evil man had collapsed on the ground. As Rossa watched, his evil heart beat slower and slower until it ceased beating altogether.

Rossa didn't need to ask if the man was dead. Daddy wore one of his hidden smiles, the sort he wore when Rossa did something funny that Mother didn't like, and he had to hide his smile from Mother.

Rossa gave a little nod. She wasn't sure how, but her father had killed the evil man. Stopped his heart dead.

One day, she vowed, she would be just like him. Evil men would fear her, and good people would come to her for help. Just like Daddy.

Three

Boris woke with the dawn, as was his habit. The war might be over for the moment, but old habits died harder than a Bisseni berserker. His wife Vica lay asleep beside him, and little Lida was curled up in her cradle in the corner. A reminder of who he fought for and why he spent so long away – protecting his wife and child, as well as all the wives and children in his father's kingdom. They deserved to sleep safely in their beds, too.

His men, camped in the fields outside Rostov, would be awake. He'd made it a habit to break his fast while walking through the camp, exchanging words with not just his knights but their men, too. He could do that this morning, and still have time to return to the house and have breakfast with Vica when she woke.

Boris dressed, not bothering to put on his armour today. What danger had he to fear here at home?

The camp bustled with activity, quite the opposite of his quiet home. A rider galloped past him, headed for the command tent in the centre. Instinct made Boris change course to follow the lathered horse. Whatever tidings the man carried, they must be urgent.

When he reached the command tent, both horse and rider had gone, but a pensive Sir Cyril stood in conference with several other knights, frowning at the missive in Cyril's hand.

"Well met, Your Highness," Sir Cyril called, spotting him first.

The other knights merely bowed and made way for him.

Boris nodded at the paper. "What news?"

The knights eyed each other, none wanting to speak the ill words aloud.

Cyril sighed. "Prince Yaroslav sends word from the north. Your father has succumbed to his illness, and your brother now sits upon the throne."

Grief caught Boris's heart in its mailed fist. "My father is dead?"

"It seems so, Your Highness. Your brother Sviatopolk is king now."

Boris started in surprise. "Sviatopolk? But I thought…"

Boris had never truly thought about which of his father's sons would take the throne upon his father's death, but for his father to name his bastard son Sviatopolk as his heir over any of his legitimate offspring seemed more than a little strange. As the oldest legitimate son, coming home from a successful military campaign, surely Boris himself would be the better choice.

Not that he wanted a throne. No, he wanted his father on the throne, so he could tell him about the campaign.

Now that tale would go untold.

"Your brother Yaroslav sent you a gift, the fruit of a successful hunt in the far north. A small token of his affection and loyalty, he says." Cyril gestured, and one of his men held out a bulky package.

Boris had no choice but to take it, and, with all eyes upon him, open it, too.

Creamy white fur spilled out, lined with lambswool. It was at once the most beautiful and the most impractical cloak Boris had ever seen. In battle, it would turn from white to red in a day, and then to black and rust after that. This was a cloak for court.

"Prince Yaroslav is coming south, to join his forces with yours so that he might set the rightful king upon the throne," Cyril said.

The rightful king was the heir his father had chosen.

Had Father really chosen Sviatopolk to be king?

"We will fight beside you, Your Majesty," Sir Cyril said, dropping to one knee. The other knights did the same.

Boris shook his head and gestured for them to get up. "I'm your prince, not your king. I will not go to war against my brother, if he is my father's chosen heir. My father was a good and wise king, and he would have made his choice with as much wisdom and forethought as any other decision he made. I must ride for Prislav immediately, to see my new king and offer him my allegiance."

"We will ride with you, Your Highness," Cyril said.

Once again, Boris shook his head. "I shall go alone. King or not, Sviatopolk is my brother. We are family. If my father chose him as king, then I am honour-bound to serve him as I served my father. As are we all. I have no need of an army at my back to speak to my brother, even if he is now my king."

"Your Highness…" Cyril was too loyal a man to say the words, but his expression said he had grave misgivings about this course of action.

Bur Boris was decided. "Send the men home to their families. We will not campaign again before spring, unless the king orders otherwise."

"Yes, Your Highness."

The knights dispersed, leaving Boris to shake his head and sigh. He'd hoped for more than a night in Vica's arms – perhaps enough nights to sire a son – but it was not to be. He was a prince first, and a husband second. First he must serve his king and his kingdom, and then he might spend a quiet winter with his wife and daughter.

Home would still be here when he returned from court.

Nodding to himself, Boris trudged home to don his travelling clothes once more.

"Ready?" Father asked.

Rossa nodded sharply. "How many targets today?" She would get them all this time, she swore. Without missing a single one.

Father tilted his head to the side, as though he needed to consider for a moment before he said, "Twelve."

Another nod, and she was off.

She caught sight of the first one, half-hidden behind a tree. She slipped around the other side of the thick trunk, then plunged her dagger into the target's neck, or where it would have been, had the target been a man and not a stuffed sack. An ambush like this one usually had more than one, in line of sight of each other...

Rossa pressed against the straw corpse, scanning the trees for his accomplice. Ah, there it was.

Carefully, she strung her bow, and took aim at the painted acorn, set high in the fork of a tree on the other side of the path. When she loosed her arrow, she didn't wait to watch it hit its target, as she knew it would. Instead, she shifted to a new position and scanned the forest for other targets.

High, low, behind trees and rocks, she took out her targets, disarming two traps and springing a third, rendering it harmless, until her count reached eleven.

One more to go.

She followed the game trail in a long loop, back to where they'd started, but she didn't see a hint of a target anywhere.

Had she missed one on her way, which now lay behind her, or had her father placed it at their meeting point, ready to ambush her when she thought she was safe?

While there were many who wished to engage the services of an assassin, hired killers were not well-liked, and their heads often fetched as high a price as the people they killed. So, her father would definitely have placed a target where it might shoot her in the back, when she reached the meeting point.

Rossa skirted the clearing, selecting a tree that would give her a good view across the dell where she knew her father waited, while its branches would hide her from the sight of anyone who might hope to catch her unawares.

Zoticus sat on a rock in the sun, calmly slicing up an apple with his dagger, before popping the slices in his mouth, one by one. The loud crunching sounds surely would have alerted any would-be assassins to his presence, and made him an easy target, but Father had so many magical protections, even Rossa wasn't sure she could fight him and win.

The twelfth target would be somewhere that gave it a clear view of the clearing, and the path Rossa would have taken, if she hadn't chosen to climb a tree. She scanned the clearing, then the treeline, then did it all again.

It had to be there. The twelfth one had to…there! Just as she saw a hint of red paint, it vanished. Yet something was there, moving along the tree branch…

She nocked an arrow to her bow, sighting along it as she exhaled. Her arrow flew across the clearing, sinking into its target before tumbling off into the undergrowth.

There. Mission complete.

Rossa slid down the tree trunk and skipped into the clearing. "I'm done, Father," she announced. She couldn't keep the pride out of her voice.

"How many did you take down?"

"All twelve."

"Ah, but you missed one," he said, rising.

On the rock he'd been sitting on, a patterned sack came into view.

Rossa knew better than to argue. He'd said twelve and she'd hit twelve, but here was a thirteenth to taunt her.

She drew her dagger and flung it at the cloth. The blade struck the centre of the target, then tipped over onto the ground, taking the sack with it.

"All thirteen," she said.

"And now you're a blade short, with only half a quiver of arrows, going to meet the contact who sent you on your quest. Not all men are honourable, and those who would hire one assassin to kill for them aren't above hiring others, so that they don't have to pay the first," Father said, drawing both daggers.

Rossa swallowed. She had one knife in easy reach, but to draw any of the others, she'd need to take her gaze off her opponent, which would be a costly mistake.

Perhaps if she could reach the sack and the knife she'd thrown…

She edged away from her father, hoping to put the stone between them before he advanced.

A shrill scream rose from the trees behind her.

"What in heaven's name – " she began.

Before she could finish, she found herself flat on her back, without the breath to say another word.

The screaming had stopped.

"This is what happens when you kill an innocent, and leave them to suffer," her father said, holding up one of her arrows, which impaled both a painted acorn and a squirrel who had tried to steal it. The limp squirrel would never scream again.

Rossa shuddered and sat up. She dragged in a breath, then said, "But it was a thief, stealing my acorn!"

"Thieves are beneath an assassin's notice. So is anyone except the target who deserves to die. Unless you are hired to kill a thief, or the thief threatens your life, he is nothing to you. Justice will find him, without your help." Father slid the squirrel's body off the arrow, and tossed it into the trees. "And you never hurt innocents."

"Thieving squirrels aren't innocent. The monks up at the castle swear about them all the time," Rossa protested.

Father just frowned. "Collect your things, then we'll return home. A good assassin…"

"Never leaves a trace," Rossa finished for him, sighing. Her father might have finished arguing with her, but she knew she hadn't won. No one could beat her father, in a fight or an argument. Least of all her.

Father inclined his head. "You have learned so much, Rossa. If I'd only known half what you do now when I was your age…" Now it was his turn not to finish his sentence. Instead, he sighed.

There was darkness in his past, from long before he met Mother, Rossa knew, but he never talked about it. She'd asked Mother, who'd told her that everyone had regrets, and her father's were for the people he could not save, which is why he had chosen his line of work in the first place.

He trained her so hard so that when her time came to exact justice, she would have no such regrets – she'd save those who needed it.

But after today's debacle, her time wouldn't be for a while yet.

Rossa sighed and tramped back along the game trail to retrieve her arrows.

Five

Dusk smudged the sky when Boris trudged up the steps to the throne room in Prislav, not pausing to take off the white fur cloak. The usual crowd of courtiers and petitioners was gone, so the king had finished hearings for the day. But the route to the royal apartments lay through the throne room, so he crossed the empty hall and kept going.

As Sviatopolk was a bastard, he'd had much more modest chambers in the palace than those given to Boris and his legitimate brothers, so it didn't surprise Boris at all to find his brother had already moved to the king's apartments.

What did surprise him was that his brother sat alone, his head and shoulders bowed with the weight of the kingdom he now carried.

"Is the crown so heavy, brother?" Boris asked.

Sviatopolk lifted his head. "Boris? Oh, you do not know how good it is to see you, brother!"

The two men embraced, and as Sviatopolk leaned against him for just that moment, Boris wondered if it was the weight of kingship he felt, a burden that was far more than one man could bear.

"How fared you in the campaign against the Bisseni?" Sviatopolk asked eagerly. "Father talked of little else in his final days. He made me swear I would not hinder you in your work, preserving our borders against those cowardly raiders. His greatest regret was not leaving a peaceful kingdom for his people."

Boris forced a smile. "The campaign ended in victory, or I should still be out there fighting them. What few Bisseni that were left fled into the mountains. They will not trouble us again for a while. And surely that cannot be all our father spoke of in his final moments. He named his heir, did he not?"

Sviatopolk shook his head.

What? A flash of triumph sparked in Boris's breast. He knew Father had not chosen Sviatopolk as his successor.

"I fear Father was too ill to know what he said at the end, for I scarcely believe it myself. In between his constant talk of you and your campaign, he made me swear to take the throne so you could stay in the field and fight. When the kingdom needs a king to make war on one front and another to sit on the throne and keep the peace with our neighbours, he had to choose, he said. So he said I should take the throne, so that you could command our armies. His final act was to declare the legitimacy of my birth, so that I might be crowned upon his death. I protested that you would make a better king, but he ordered me to be silent unless I wanted to go to war in your place. Heaven knows I am no warrior."

Sviatopolk laughed.

As a bastard born of the king and a serving girl, Sviatopolk's blood had not been considered noble enough to cross swords with the other princes and young noblemen in the practice yard. Yet now he was the highest man in the land, with no sword skills to speak of. No, Sviatopolk would not have survived even his first battle against the Bisseni.

"So it is true? Father named you as his heir?" Boris pressed.

"For my sins, yes. I wish he had chosen someone better suited, but how can any son deny his father one last dying request?" Sviatopolk's eyes appeared haunted for a just a moment, before he managed a smile. "But you are here, and victorious, too, so we must have a feast to celebrate. I'll send word to the kitchens, and you shall sit at my right hand at the high table, so that we may drink to our father's memory, and the peace he did not live to see."

"I would be honoured, Your Majesty. And on the morrow, I will swear fealty to you, before the whole court," Boris said. His brother would not lie about such things. His father had chosen him to be king, with Boris as his general. Indeed, how could any dutiful son deny his father's last request?

Family did not betray family, after all.

Six

When Rossa sat down to dinner, she found her whole family present – including her half brother, Tobias, and his wife and children. Was it some important feast day, that she'd forgotten? She'd been so intent on her training, one day blended into another until even Sundays took her by surprise.

"Aren't you going to wish me a happy birthday?" Rossa's nephew, Bruno, demanded.

Ah, so that was the occasion.

Rossa shrugged. As her brother's only son and heir, Bruno was fussed over most days, so she felt little need to add to his over-inflated sense of self-importance.

"You're a terrible aunt," Bruno complained. "On my friend Peter's birthday, his spinster aunt gave him a whole new set of clothes, and new boots, with a purse of coins to hang from his new belt. And she spent a whole week before his birthday, cooking all his favourite foods."

"Peter the innkeeper's son?" Rossa asked. At Bruno's nod, she continued, "Dominique is not a spinster. She's a Rialto courtesan, who spends more money on potions from Swanhild and Raphael than the rest of Mirroten combined. Peter's new clothes were likely not new at all, but left behind by one of her clients." Rossa suspected Dominique would have quite the story to tell about the client who'd lost his clothes – she'd have to ask her to regale the tale when she next came home.

Bruno's brow creased with puzzlement. Evidently his education had not included herbalism, or the customs and courtesans of Rialto. "You're still a mean aunt," he announced, before stuffing his face with food.

Assassins were not known for their kindness, so she said, "Good," before she reached for the meat.

Bruno swallowed with difficulty. "Peter says you're going to be a spinster because no one wants to marry you. You should be married already, he says."

"Peter says, or his older brother John says?" Rossa asked sharply. Though she wouldn't have put it past either of them to be making snide comments about her, after she'd repeatedly turned down invitations from both boys for most of the spring and summer. Last year, it had just been John, but now Peter was the ripe age of fourteen, he deemed himself enough of a man to pester her, too.

"They say if you don't marry soon, no one will have you, for all the good men will be taken," Bruno said. "You spend too much time in the forest alone. You'll never be as good as Master Zoticus. Better to be a proper wife and have babies. Some of them say you can't have babies because you're a witch, an evil witch."

Oh, that part was too good. "Ah, but I am a witch," she purred, wiggling her fingers. "Want to see if I can turn you into a slug without anyone noticing?"

"Mother!" The wail that came out of Bruno sounded like it came from a boy much younger than ten.

Conversation around the table stilled.

"What is it?" Silvana asked, the edge on her tone sharp enough to cut through bone. She didn't spoil her son, though Tobias did.

"Aunt Rossa said she'd turn me into a slug!"

"What did you say to her?"

"I only said what everyone says – she should hurry up and get married!"

Silvana's lips thinned. "And?"

Rossa recognised the danger in her sister in law's tone, even if Silvana's own son didn't.

"If she doesn't pick a husband soon, she'll turn into an evil old witch!"

Silvana pointed at the door. "Lady Sara needs more kindling for the fire. Go outside and chop some for her. Now."

"But it's my birthday, and I haven't finished my dinner," Bruno whined.

"Do as your mother says, boy. Are you sure you're ten, if you haven't even learned that yet?" Father only had to look at Bruno for the boy to shrink. "What are you waiting for?"

Bruno bolted outside. Soon, Rossa could hear the sounds of an axe at work.

Silvana shook her head. "I'm sorry, Rossa, he's become impossible of late. Before the twins died, they kept him in order, but after…" She stared at Mother. "Was Tobias ever this much trouble?"

Mother laughed. "Tobias was never any trouble. He's always been his father's son, and if I hadn't been there at his birth, I'd wonder how such a placid child could have ever been mine. However, I do remember your father was quite the troublemaker. The things he used to get up to with my brothers…"

All dead now, Rossa knew.

"What the boy needs is some discipline and responsibility. Have you tried goats?" Father asked.

Mother bit back a smile, but no one else dared to laugh.

Tobias looked uncomfortable. "Since the avalanche took both his brothers, he won't go anywhere near the goats. He's terrified of them

– has been since he was little, and one of them butted him so hard, he couldn't sit for a week."

Now it was Rossa's turn to smile. The boy had been taunting the goats, and she might have given the goat's horns a little magical help.

"You should have sent Bruno off to become a knight," Rossa said. In her father's stories, all knights deserved to be turned into slugs. Though he'd exacted a more permanent kind of justice on them, as was fitting for a man of his talents.

"He's a little old to be a pageboy, yet too young to be a squire. Maybe…" Mother said, staring at Father. "Would you know a knight who would train him?"

Father looked thoughtful. "Several, actually, but I think he'd do best with the Baron of Maraschal. He owes me a favour for returning one of his breeding mares, among other things."

Rossa opened her mouth to ask for the tale, but her mother pointed at Tobias's two young daughters, and shook her head. Rossa shut her mouth with a snap, and resolved to ask him later.

"What sort of man is the Baron?" Tobias asked.

Father shrugged. "The Baron I knew is likely dead and buried by now, and one of his sons has taken his place. They were all honourable men, riding all over their family lands to settle disputes and see that their people were well defended. Their money comes from the exquisite horses they breed, local stock mixed with horses one of their ancestors brought back from the very first crusade, though they have some contacts in the Holy Land still. His daughter…why, I see her like in Rossa here. Young Melisende joined a crusade herself once, and held her own in battle, but she was a trained healer when she was at home, seeing to the health of all her father's people." Father grinned. "All the family work hard, especially when it comes to the horses. Bruno will learn to behave as a proper young baron should, or he'll spend his days shovelling horse shit."

Tobias didn't look convinced, but Silvana nodded sharply. "Will you write a letter to the

Baron, please, Master Zoticus? The sooner we send Bruno to train, the better."

Father inclined his head. "You shall have it by morning, as long as Sara remembered to buy more ink from the traders today."

"Of course I remembered. I'm not so old that I would forget to visit any traders who come so far up the river. They would not let me forget, either – you spend more coin than the rest of the town combined." Mother sucked in a breath. "Oh, I almost forgot. A message came for you, too. I didn't dare break the seal on the scroll."

A frown crossed Father's face, before serenity reigned there again. "I'll read it after dinner. Whatever they want can wait."

Mother looked like she wanted to argue, but she stayed silent. Whoever's emblem she'd seen on the seal must be important. A king, an emperor...or perhaps the Pope? Father travelled less and less now, but he still took on some assignments. He might have more white hair than brown, but he was still a formidable fighter any man would fear.

One day, she'd be good enough to go with

him. But if she asked today, she knew what the answer would be. He no longer said a simple, "No," anymore – he'd ask her if she thought she was ready to be an assassin, to take someone's life while keeping a firm hand on her own, yet to do it so subtly, so carefully, that no one but she would know she had done the deed.

If it weren't for that thieving squirrel…

Rossa sighed. One day. But not today, or tomorrow, either.

Seven

"To the late king, my father. May his place in heaven be assured!" Sviatopolk shouted, raising his cup.

Boris joined him in the toast, as did most of the courtiers in the feasting hall. Once again, his cup was empty. This would not have happened when Kyrilu was his squire, but Igor still had much to learn.

Boris gestured for a servant to fill his cup. After some time, Igor appeared, looking sulky, but carrying a pitcher of ale.

"A squire should be more attentive, boy.

This is not the first time my cup has been empty. The king has proposed many toasts tonight, and if I had to refuse to drink on account of having an empty cup, it would be a terrible slight to my brother. Why, better men have been tried for treason, bringing such dishonour to their king!" Boris said, thrusting his cup forward.

"Perhaps if you did not drink so much, Your Highness," Igor said. "If you were more careful about what you drink – "

Boris slammed his hand on the table. "I will not be lectured to by my squire. I can hold my drink as well as any man here, and you'd do well to remember your station. Your job is to keep my cup filled, and if you do not, I shall find myself a better squire who can!"

Igor winced. "But, Your Highness – "

"Fill my cup or get out of my sight!"

Igor filled the cup, and Boris drained it, then held it out for more.

"Again!"

The look on Igor's face was one of pure pain, as though pouring the drink cut him to the core. Yet he did as he was commanded, before slinking away.

None too soon, for Sviatopolk was on his feet again, raising his cup to Boris.

"My late father said this kingdom must have both a ruler and a protector, and he was blessed to have sons who could do both. United, Prince Boris and I will bring a peace to this kingdom even my wise father could not. I pledge the health of Prince Boris. May we celebrate many more of his victories, against the Bisseni and any other enemy who dares to threaten us!" Sviatopolk roared.

Roars of agreement came from around the hall as everyone drank Boris's health.

He felt his face grow hot. His king had praised him, and he had not yet toasted his new king's health. He must make amends.

Boris rose up onto unsteady feet. The ale was strong tonight – he had not drunk too much of it, no matter what his squire said.

"To our new king. Long may he reign!" Boris said. He lifted his cup, then drained it in one big gulp.

The other men in the hall thundered their approval, shouts and stomps ringing from the very rafters as they drank to their king's health.

Boris sat down suddenly, finding his legs would no longer hold him up.

The ale must be terribly strong, for he could not remember being this drunk since…

The world went black.

Eight

When day dawned, Father had already left, and Mother had that steely look in her eye that said anyone who disobeyed her would rue it for the rest of their life.

So when Mother said, "We must finish shelling the chestnuts today," Rossa merely nodded and resigned herself to a day at home.

At least she'd be spared Bruno's company – Father had written the letter he'd promised, and Tobias and Silvana were preparing him for the journey to the Baron of Maraschal's lands. Tobias would take him on the morrow, and hope to be home before winter.

Rossa finished her breakfast, and headed for the smokehouse. The sooner she started, the sooner she'd be finished for the day. Maybe there'd be enough light to squeeze in some archery practice, when the chestnuts were done.

Mother had taught her to choose chestnuts the way her mother and grandmother had taught her, weighing each in her hand as she picked them. So Rossa knew what to look for when she sat in the middle of the smokehouse and summoned her magic.

Four baskets drifted into a line before her, ready and waiting. Rossa took a deep breath and sent her awareness out through the smokehouse. The ripest, ready to be released from their shells, rose from the racks where they'd been smoking for weeks, and floated to the nearest basket. Within moments, all four baskets were filled to the brim.

Rossa took two baskets in each hand, and headed outside to the table overlooking the lake that gave Mirroten its name.

"Good morning! I thought you'd be in the

forest, training with your father," Swanhild said, already seated and waiting.

Rossa forced out a smile. "A message came for Father yesterday, so he left for urgent business this morning." She pulled off her soft slippers and tugged on her boots.

Swanhild's grin was as natural as the sky above. "Ooh, I wonder who his business involves."

"He's gone to the Emperor's court in Byzas. It could be anybody," Mother said, dumping the first basket of chestnuts into the pressing tub.

Rossa didn't wait for her to ask — she stepped into the tub and started crushing the shells with her heavy boots. Usually Silvana did this, but not today.

"So, do you think he's going to assassinate the Emperor, or work for him?" Swanhild asked.

"In that court, anything's possible, but from what he said last night, I suspect he's tangled in a squabble between two members of the royal family. He wants us to spend the winter up at the castle, just in case," Mother said.

Rossa stepped out of the tub, so that her mother could divide the crushed chestnuts between the baskets for peeling.

"I told him we'd go as soon as the chestnuts are sent to the mill," Mother finished.

Rossa's breath caught in her throat. Spending a whole winter at the castle in the mountains? She hadn't done that since she was a small child, hiding from the plague that had swept up the river, wiping out whole villages.

"Is Silvana going, too?" Swanhild asked.

"No, she's staying to take care of the town. Truly, I should pass the title to her and Tobias now, if I had any sense, and retire from the town council and everything." Mother's hands moved so quickly, prying the nuts loose from their shells, then tossing the nuts into one sack and the shells into a tub at her feet.

Swanhild laughed. "My mother would turn over in her grave to hear you say that! It wouldn't be Mirroten without Mistress Sara ruling over us all, she would say, before telling some story about how you terrified a grown man into doing your bidding. She would have loved to see you tame Master Zoticus."

That set Mother laughing, too. "Zoticus is the sort of man who can never be tamed. I never thought he could be content staying here in Mirroten, and he has gone away on his missions, as he calls them, yet he always returns to me. Maybe that's why Rossa hasn't fallen for any of the boys in town. She yearns for someone untameable, like I did."

"Is that true, Rossa?" Swanhild asked. "Is that why you spend so much time in the forest – looking for a wild man to take as your lover?"

Rossa choked. "I go hunting in the forest with my father!" They never encountered anyone else, except occasionally Swanhild, when the healer was out collecting herbs.

"So you don't know where the clearing with the ancient altar is? Remind me to show you sometime," Swanhild said, mischief twinkling in her eyes. "It would not do if you got lost on your way there with your wild lover."

"Don't say such things in front of my mother!" Rossa hissed.

"Your mother, who has gone quite a telling shade of red? Oh, Mistress Sara knows exactly where her ancestors performed their ancient fertility rites, for she's the one who showed my mother, who passed the knowledge on to me. If I'm not mistaken, your brother Tobias was likely conceived before that very altar."

Mother rose. "I'm going to get more nuts." She hurried off to the smokehouse.

Swanhild smiled. "There, now she's gone…what's his name? Your lover in the woods?"

"I'm not in love with anyone!" Rossa cried, clenching her fists. Magic bubbled up within her. If she shed so much as a drop of blood, she'd sent the whole table flying, chestnuts and all. She fought to control it.

"That's because the man for you is not here. He's…" Swanhild closed her eyes and bit her lip, sparking her own magic into life. She sat there in silence for a long moment before her eyes popped open. "Ooh, I can feel him, though he's far away. Over the mountains. At the castle, maybe, or the monastery? Maybe you will seduce a monk. Enchant him so completely, he forgets his vows of celibacy and pledges himself to your pleasure instead…"

Now Rossa's cheeks grew hot. "I would never ask a man to break his vows. And I could never love someone so dishonourable."

"Maybe a courtier, then? The king's court lies that way, across the mountains, too. When the winter is over, your mother might send you to court. You are a lady, after all. A pity there is no queen at the moment, or I would suggest your mother send you to be one of her ladies in waiting. Plenty of men you might meet when you keep company with a queen." Swanhild's smile faltered a little.

She had spent time at court, before she married Raphael, the town apothecary, Rossa remembered. "Was that what you were?" she asked eagerly. "A lady in waiting?"

Swanhild shuddered. "No, I was…more like the queen's ward, for a time. Before she came to a tragic end. The king never did remarry. A most…unfortunate affair."

Rossa opened her mouth to ask for Swanhild to tell the whole tale, instead of just this tantalising glimpse.

"What is unfortunate?" Mother demanded, tipping a new basket of nuts into the pressing tub.

"Oh, I was just saying to Rossa that it is unfortunate we have no queen, or she could go to court to meet her wild man," Swanhild said. She grew thoughtful. "If he's a courtier, he would have to be most refined in the king's presence, and keep his wildness for the hunt or the bedchamber. You'd have to accompany a hunting party to see him truly in his element, I imagine."

Rossa fought her rising panic. She didn't want a man in her bedchamber.

"Zoticus would never allow his daughter to go to court without him," Sara said. "No suitor would dare look at her with him around."

Rossa dared to breathe again.

"Don't be silly. Rossa will fall for a man who not only has the courage to stand before her father, but who does not fear him." Swanhild held out her empty basket for Rossa to fill.

"But I don't…I won't…" Rossa began.

Mother burst out laughing. "There isn't a man alive who isn't afraid of my Zoticus. And if there is, he's a fool. Rossa would not choose to marry a fool."

"I don't want to marry anyone!" Rossa said hotly.

Swanhild patted her hand. "Of course not. None of us want to be bothered by a man, until the right man gets down on his knees. It usually takes him a few tries to work out what to do with his tongue, if he's not that experienced, but once you've trained him…"

"You're as salty as your mother!" Mother swore.

"I'm going to get more nuts," Rossa said, heading for the smokehouse.

Neither woman noticed, for they were too busy talking about…unspeakable things. At length. With obscene hand gestures and way too much laughter.

Nine

The sound of screaming sent daggers through Boris's head. By all that was holy, why had he drunk so much? And why in heaven's name must they scream so?

"Enough, woman," he grumbled.

But the screams only grew louder. He fancied he could hear his name amid the wordless shrieks.

Boris forced his eyes open, and felt as if the light were stabbing them, too. The light of a single torch lit the stone room, but it was enough to see a pair writhing on the floor together.

"Go bed the girl in your own chamber," Boris grumbled, lifting his hand to shade his eyes.

Or at least he tried to, but he couldn't seem to reach. His hand stopped short, and he squinted to see why. A manacle encased his wrist, fastened to a chain that he assumed was fixed to the wall behind him. His other hand bore a metal cuff, too, and equally heavy chains.

"Boris! Help me!"

Boris blinked. Vica? Some other man was bedding Vica? He roared and tried to reach them, but his chain was too short.

His struggles attracted the man's attention, though, so he left Vica alone to stride over to Boris. The stranger wore the livery of the castle guards, though he was no one Boris knew.

Boris's eyes darted to Vica. Blood stained the front of her slashed gown, and tears streaked her cheeks, which already darkened with a blooming bruise no doubt inflicted by the villainous guard advancing on him.

"I will have you executed for daring to touch the Princess of Rostov," Boris declared, glaring at the man.

"Me and the princess are busy," the man declared, throwing a punch at Boris.

Between the mother of all hangovers and his chains, Boris was too slow to dodge the blow. Instead, the man sent him reeling against the wall, and the impact sent him back into the darkness, followed by the sound of Vica's screams.

Ten

It was late afternoon by the time Mother called a halt to peeling chestnuts, so she and Swanhild might make dinner. Rossa escaped before she was forced to help with the cooking, too. She'd rather be out in the forest, hunting fresh meat for the stewpot, than hunched over the stewpot, stirring it.

After all day sitting in the autumn sun, the coolness in the shade of the forest was as refreshing as the waterskin of well-water she'd brought with her. Rossa's feet found their own way back to the clearing where she'd last trained with Father.

Where a single squirrel had been her downfall.

The squirrel's corpse still lay where it had fallen, cold and stiff after a night on the ground. She bit her lip and sent a bolt of magic into the dead squirrel. The sort of magic she didn't dare practice in town, or where anyone might see her.

The squirrel moved, stiffly at first, then more like the living creature it had once been as the magic began to work.

"Take to the trees," Rossa whispered to it.

The squirrel scampered up the nearest tree trunk, then broke into a run across the branches above Rossa's head.

She dug her teeth into her lip again, conjuring missiles made of magic alone. One by one, she directed the dagger-shaped projectiles at the fast-moving squirrel. And again, and again…

The magic blades passed harmlessly though the enchanted squirrel, before splashing on the leaves and branches behind it. The magic crackled and spat for a moment, before it vanished, leaving the trees relatively unharmed.

It did not have to be so – she could conjure fireballs, blades of ice or bolts of magic so concentrated, they punched holes through things. Father sometimes permitted her to practice with magical projectiles, but he preferred her to be proficient in more mundane weapons, leaving her magic for a last resort. A secret weapon, ready to be called upon when she needed it.

She'd tried using her magic against her father once in a fight, and only succeeded in knocking herself out when the spell rebounded, magnified, thanks to one of the magical charms he wore. She'd since managed to replicate such a shield around herself – no charm needed – but it had taken the shape of a large bubble, a sword's length from her body, so that it stopped her from fighting at all.

As the waning evening light would, too.

Rossa sighed. Her mother expected her home by nightfall. Never mind that there was nothing in this forest that was a match for her magic – her mother's word was law, and Rossa knew better than to disobey.

Besides, if she was late for dinner, there might be nothing left — Mother had been known to give their leftovers to the less fortunate in town. Especially if they were headed up into the mountains soon.

Rossa took a moment to dispel the spell on the squirrel, then buried the creature's corpse in a shallow grave beside the tree it had originally fallen from. Thief or no, it had helped her today, however unwittingly. And yesterday, for her father was right — she did need to be vigilant, not just for thieves, but for innocents who did not deserve to die.

Tomorrow, she would do better. And with that thought, Rossa straightened her shoulders and strode home.

Eleven

When Boris awoke, the chains were gone. Had he dreamed them?

A straw pallet crackled beneath him as he rolled over, sliding out from under what he recognised as his white cloak and onto the cold stone floor. The blinding headache he'd had in his dream was little more than a memory.

And Vica…

No, Vica was home in Rostov, where she belonged, with Lida. He could not have seen her here in Prislav, with some other man.

He drew in a deep breath and let it out

slowly, before taking another.

It smelled like a battlefield in here. Had Igor neglected to clean his armour again?

"Igor? Where are you, boy?" Boris demanded.

"I'm here, Your Highness." The boy appeared, his eyes wide with what looked like terror.

If the boy would only do his job, he wouldn't have to fear punishment, but Boris didn't say it aloud. Let the boy figure it out for himself.

"Fetch me something to eat and drink," Boris said. "And then clean my armour."

The boy swallowed. "I…I can't, Your Highness. I can only give you this." He held out a bottle, small enough to fit in the boy's closed fist. "I'm to tell you if you wish to live to seek vengeance, you must drink this. Word reached us today that your brother David is dead, too. Cut down as he prayed for your father's soul in the chapel."

David was dead? But David was just a boy, and his only surviving full-blood brother, sent to a monastery to spend his life serving the church. No one could possibly want to murder David, and what man would kill a prince at prayer?

"Your brother did this. If you want vengeance, you must drink this," Igor insisted.

Boris's wits were slow, but those he'd begun to gather told him not to trust Igor. He dashed the bottle from the boy's hand, and it fell into the straw. "I'll drink no more of your poison, traitor. You gave me the tainted ale at the feast."

The boy bowed his head, but he did not deny it.

"Tell me where I might find my wife."

Boris prayed she was safe at Rostov, where she belonged.

The boy's eyes grew wide. He swallowed. Words seemed to fail him as he raised a shaking hand to point across the room. "She's there, Your Highness."

So he had not dreamed it. Vica was here.

"Get out," Boris snarled at the boy.

Igor scrambled away, bolting through the door before slamming it behind him.

Boris sat up, and, when his head did not

threaten to explode, he rose to his feet.

A bundle of bloody clothes lay in the corner, as though someone had flung them there.

Please, let it not be her.

He forced himself to step closer. One step. Another. A third. Until he was close enough to turn the bundle over.

By all that was holy…

No, by all that was unholy.

Vica's mouth hung open in a silent scream, likely at the dagger buried in her breast that had stopped her heart. Her lifeblood stained her gown in rusty brown, wet and cold, for her spirit had fled many hours ago, while he'd lain senseless.

He shifted her body until he laid her out on the stone floor, then folded her arms across her breast. He should take the dagger out, and use it to take the life of his wife's murderer.

But what did he know about the man, aside from the guard uniform he'd worn?

Boris scanned the room, looking for some clue to the man's identity.

Only then did he see the second, smaller

bundle.

His arms reached out of their own accord, before even his mind could stop him.

The bastard who'd killed his wife had cut Lida's throat, slicing so deep, he'd almost taken the little girl's head off.

Boris fell to his knees, cradling his daughter's mangled body to his chest, and wept.

$$Twelve$$

An eternity might have passed, or it could have only been a moment. Boris wasn't sure it mattered any more. He laid Lida's body beside her mother's, hands folded at her breast like the angel she surely was now.

He stared down at what had been his family, wishing with all his heart that he was with them now.

It would be so easy…

He had only to take the dagger from Vica's breast, still coated with the blood that had once given her so much life, and plunge it into his own heart. Two hearts, together forever.

The dagger felt so light in his hand, as cold as the death that awaited him, just one sharp thrust away.

But the balance was off…this was some other man's knife, an inferior blade to his own. Boris threw it down, and it clattered across the stone floor to land in the straw pallet he'd slept on.

David would have shaken his head, and told him it was a sin to take your own life. If Boris killed himself, he'd never see Vica and Lida again.

Or David, who was dead, too.

Dead by his brother's hand, if Igor was to be believed. Was his brother responsible for Vica's death, too? And little Lida, who had never been a threat to anyone?

The only brother here in Prislav who could have had a hand in their death was Sviatopolk. Their cursed new king.

His brother's betrayal stabbed him sharper than any knife. No, Sviatopolk was no brother of his. Not kin or blood or anything to him. He was as destined for death as any Bisseni raider who dared set foot on their kingdom's soil

Vica, David, Lida…had Sviatopolk killed their father, too? Such a vile traitor might do anything to secure the throne.

But he would not have it, Boris vowed. He cursed Sviatopolk's name, and cursed that he'd ever called the worm brother.

No more.

He'd bury the inferior blade in his brother's breast, and make him bleed. For Vica.

Boris headed for the pile of straw where he'd last seen the dagger. He donned the cloak, still miraculously white in a room so steeped in blood. Then he clawed though the bed, desperate to find the blade, but his hand closed around a bottle instead.

The bottle Igor had given him. For vengeance.

Boris uncorked it, and sniffed at the contents.

Liquid sloshed, sending the scent of bitter herbs wafting up his nose.

Vengeance did not smell like much more than a simple tonic, if that's what this was.

Yet there were poisons that could not be discerned by smell alone, like whatever Igor had put into his ale at the feast.

Ale Igor had told him not to drink, now he remembered. Did that mean this new elixir would help set things right?

Or send his soul spiralling up to heaven to rejoin his wife and daughter?

Carefully, Boris corked the bottle and set it on the floor.

He took a cloth and washed his wife's face, then did the same for his daughter. Long he looked at them, memorising every detail, for if he succeeded in this, he might never see them again.

But it would be worth it, to know they were avenged, and their souls could rest.

Until they were, his soul would never rest.

He leaned over and kissed Lida's cheek, like he'd done so many times before.

Never again.

Swallowing, he moved to kneel beside Vica, Princess Slavica of Rostov, a woman he'd been blessed to call his wife, if only for a little while. He touched his lips to hers, wishing fate had allowed them one last kiss. For letting her die instead of defending her, he did not deserve one, but men have always wished for more than they deserved, he knew.

Boris uncorked the bottle, and raised it high. "For you. For David and Lida and my father, but most of all for you, Vica. May your place in heaven be assured, as I send the man responsible for all this to hell."

He drank.

The potion was barely a mouthful, yet it burned his mouth like molten metal, coating his throat in liquid fire until he could not even scream at the agony.

Still it burned, invading his blood, spreading through his body like wildfire, until he could bear the pain no more and the world went white.

Thirteen

They hadn't been on the road for three days when Rossa noticed the first flakes of white on her horse's mane. "Mother, it's snowing," she said in wonder, holding out her hand to catch some.

Mother frowned. "It's far too early for snow. We must ride faster, to get there before the pass closes."

Reluctantly, Rossa put her glove back on and urged her mare to pick up the pace.

It was still snowing when they stopped for the night, settling in white drifts anywhere that was open to the sky. Mother found a clear spot under some trees to pitch their tent, and Rossa set to work. Everything was fine until she backed into a tree branch that dumped a load of snow on her.

Rossa swore, then bit her lip and cast a shield, pushing it out a few yards to encompass the tent, her mother and the fire her mother was attempting to light. "Stay," she told it.

And it did, like a big, invisible, dome-shaped tent that kept the snow out. It slid down the sides, instead, until it formed a wall high enough for Mother to notice.

"Did you do that?" she asked, wiping a sooty hand across her brow. The firepit remained ominously dark.

Rossa nodded. "I can light the fire for you, too, if you like. Just…don't tell Father."

Mother rose clumsily from her crouch. "And why in heaven's name would I not?"

Rossa ducked her head. "Because he doesn't think magic should be used for mundane things. Cookfires and pitching tents and things that most people do without magic. He says…"

"Your father says a lot of things. And while I admit he knows more about magic than me, given both his mother and sister were enchantresses like you, I've seen him use magic for plenty of mundane things. In fact, every fire he's ever lit while travelling uses a magic candle that his mother gave him when he was a boy. A candle he keeps in his magic travelling bag, with all manner of other things." Mother sighed. "Perhaps he means that you should not take your magic for granted, to use such power without thinking about it first. To consider whether to use magic, or to stay your hand. My friend Tola, Swanhild's mother, always thought twice before using magic, because her husband used to beat her if he caught her casting a spell. Even after he died, she'd hesitate. She still warded her shop, though, and she used her magic to save Swanhild, though it cost her own life, in the end." She wiped away tears. "Oh, look at me, crying over the dead, though it's been nigh on twenty years since I last saw her. More, maybe, as it was before you were born. The last thing we talked about was your father, and how she thought I should…give him a chance."

If she was anything like Swanhild, Tola had probably said something far more crude than that. But she'd been Mother's friend, and Mother still mourned her, so Rossa kept her thoughts to herself.

"Your father slept in the tower room, and then Raphael did, when Zoticus moved into my chambers. I thought you might like the tower for yourself, this time. I sent word up to the castle to have rooms prepared for us, so it should be ready for you. But if you don't like it, I'm sure we can move your things somewhere else," Mother said.

Rossa remembered the tower room, and how Raphael would lift her up to see out the windows so she could gaze out over the countryside. When she was little, it had seemed like watching the whole world. Something God might do, and not mere mortals like her. Now, she knew she hadn't even seen the full extent of her mother's lands.

Mother, who knelt in the dirt to light her own fire, to cook their meal, because it never occurred to her to rely on servants to do what she could do herself.

As long as she didn't expect Rossa to cook. At best, she'd burn everything to cinders, and at worst, she'd poison them all, herself included. The last time she'd tried, Father had caught her in time to keep her from killing anyone. He'd said she was just like her aunt, who couldn't cook, either, and told Mother to keep Rossa out of the kitchen.

"I'm sure the tower room will be fine," Rossa said. It wasn't like she'd spend much time there, during her waking hours. She'd be training, much like she did at home. Because when her father returned, she intended to be ready. "Shall I light that fire for you now?"

Fourteen

Earth and damp and…was that wet dog he smelled? Wet fur, anyway, musky and earthy, like he'd been hunting too long in the forest.

Hunting?

Boris opened his eyes to darkness. No, dimness, for he could faintly see the outlines of walls that no sane builder would ever knowingly construct. Things stuck out of the wall and ceiling and sometimes even the floor, jagged like teeth that intended to devour him when the monster whose mouth he'd stumbled into developed an appetite.

Was he in hell, then?

No, hell would be hotter, instead of just a pleasant temperature.

He lay in a cave, then, upon a pile of half-rotted leaves, with a stream trickling in the darkness, real darkness, deeper inside. Now, if he could only find the dog…

Boris scanned the cave.

There, in the corner. Something that might be an emaciated dog, curled up in exhaustion, a bag of bones clinging to life.

Boris approached cautiously, not wanting to scare the beast so that it would bite.

Yet the closer he got, the less it looked like a dog, or any animal at all. A bag of bones, perhaps, but their owner had departed life a long time ago.

Boris picked up the sack and emptied it onto the ground. Metal clunked and clanged into a pile at his feet, catching what little light there was like no bones he'd ever seen.

Atop the pile was a crown he'd only ever seen on his father's head, on special events. His mother's crown lay in the tangle of items, too, along with what looked like a collection of the crown jewels.

Sviatopolk might sit on the throne, but he would never wear his father's crown, Boris thought with satisfaction.

The rightness of this thought, combined with the memory of his own hands stuffing the crowns into the sack, told him he'd been the one to steal these things, and he'd planned it to spite his brother.

Everything else was hazy, though, until he'd woken up here. His last clear memory was of drinking Igor's potion, which hadn't poisoned him after all.

Ah, but he'd said someone had ordered him to give Boris the potion, hadn't he? That mean Igor hadn't prepared the draught himself, and likely had no idea what it would do when Boris drank it.

A dog whined.

Boris shifted to a crouch, reaching for a sword that wasn't at his side, where it should be. He cursed his own stupidity for stealing the crown jewels, yet forgetting to procure a sword.

Another whine, as shadows crowded at the

cave's entrance.

Not one wet dog, but a pack of them.

The thought had barely coalesced in his mind before Boris realised his mistake.

They weren't dogs at all, but a pack of wolves.

He scrabbled at his belt, only to realise that not only had he forgotten his sword, he'd neglected to don a belt, too. It was a blessing he'd remembered to put on clothing at all, for without the thick fur garments he wore, he'd surely freeze to death in the chilly autumn evening.

One wolf stepped forward, the leader of this war band, and it gave a snarl.

Boris stared at it, reaching down for the jewelled sceptre his father had once told him had been a gift from the Emperor of Byzas.

He prayed that his father, and the long-dead emperor who had given this gift, would grant his arm and the sceptre the strength to defeat these enemies, so that he might survive to take the crown jewels somewhere safe.

The wolf leaped.

Boris swung the sceptre.

The wolf flew over its packmates and straight out of the cave.

The rest of the wolves attacked as one.

Afterwards, Boris couldn't say what had happened. He'd felt rage and a haze had come down over his eyes, and when he'd been able to think again, two wolves lay dead at his feet, while a third tried to drag itself away when both of its back legs were clearly broken.

Boris considered the injured wolf for a moment, then seized the sceptre and brought it down upon the beast's head, ending its pain. No animal deserved to suffer so.

Only when he was certain the third beast was dead did he go back to examine the other two. Both bore deep claw marks, like some great beast had slashed at them until they'd punctured something vital. Yet the only beasts Boris had seen were the wolves themselves, which did not have claws like that.

If anything, he'd think a lion had been here.

Boris tried not to laugh. There were stories of lions in far-off lands, but he'd never seen one outside of books.

He shook his head and headed out of the

cave, hoping he might wash the sceptre in the stream. It wouldn't do to have the crown jewels caked in blood.

He followed the tiny stream down the hill, until it widened into a pool big enough to immerse the sceptre in. He leaned over, wondering at the hulking shape he saw reflected in the water.

By all that was holy, it was a –

Boris overbalanced and fell in, shattering the reflection and driving all thoughts from his mind, except the most immediate question of how not to drown.

Fifteen

It was almost dark when they finally reached the castle, but the gates were open and the courtyard was filled with torches, lighting their way in.

"Lady Sara, it is an honour!" a woman said, bobbing a curtsy, and the shadowy figures behind her did the same.

"Salacia? It has been too long!" Mother, never one to stand on ceremony, hugged the woman. "What have you been doing all these years?"

"Well, after running the boarding house for

the construction crew who built the new monastery, I married one of the masons who had a secret talent for brewing beer. We turned the boarding house into an inn for pilgrims who come to see the relics. Since they saved Mirroten from the plague, many more miracles are hoped for, and not a day passes without half a dozen pilgrims arriving. Well, until the winter closes the passes, which looks like it might happen early this year. That's had a lot of people heading home, so I've left my daughters to take care of the kitchens there while I claim the castle kitchens again." Salacia grinned. "I nearly cried when I reached the cellars – so much to choose from! And always the very best."

Mother frowned. "Has the harvest been poor here this year? Or are the monks taking too much? You have only to send word down to Mirroten. We would not let you go hungry."

Salacia laughed. "Oh, no, 'tis not that, Lady Sara. But the best of the harvest always goes to the castle cellars. It's tradition. There's plenty left for the rest of us – even the pilgrims who come to see the relics at Holy Innocents on the Lake, as they call it. No, it's that the pilgrims expect plain food, not the fancy stuff that I used to make in the castle kitchens. With wine and spices and honeyed fruits from Rialto…why, it's almost like Christmas come early, though it's months off yet. But what am I saying? You must be tired from your journey. I'll have warm water sent up to your chamber and dinner will be on the table when you come down."

"Rossa can bathe and change in my chamber for now, as she used to," Mother said. "Right, Rossa?"

Rossa nodded.

Salacia's eyes widened as she stared at Rossa. "Why, I had it in my head that you would be little Lady Rossa, just like I remembered, not a real lady, old enough to be wed! Beg pardon, milady." She dropped another curtsy, considerably lower than the one she'd given Mother.

A real lady, old enough to wed. No, she was neither of those things. And if Mother could hug the woman, then Rossa was allowed to be informal, too.

Rossa summoned a smile. "Please, don't, um, Mistress Salacia. No one at home calls me that. I'm just Rossa. And no wedding for a while yet." If ever, she added silently.

Salacia beamed. "You're just like your mother. You should call me Sal, like you did when you were a little girl." She rubbed her hands together with what Rossa suspected was glee. "Ooh, you wait until some of the boys in the village see you! They'll fall all over themselves to impress you, I'm sure."

Rossa's smile faltered. That was the last thing she needed. "I'll go up and wash, I think."

"Of course, of course." Sal shooed her inside.

Thankfully, Rossa knew the way up to the tower. When she reached the top of the stairs, she opened the window, scooped up a bucket of snow, and melted it with a well-placed fireball. More than melted it, what with those wisps of steam curling up from the water.

She washed quickly, wishing she could immerse her whole body in hot water, but that would have to wait until she found a suitable tub, and carried enough water up those stairs to fill it, as there wasn't enough snow on the windowsill to fill more than a bucket or two.

Rossa brought in what she could, then closed the shutters. It was too dark to see anything out there now, and the snow was still falling.

She surveyed her tower room, which felt smaller now than it had all those years ago. Perhaps it was the carved bed that took up most of the floor space – Raphael's narrow pallet had been enough for him then. Had he and Swanhild ever…?

Shuddering, Rossa trotted down the stairs for dinner, trying to shake such distasteful thoughts out of her head.

$\mathcal{S}ixteen$

"Where's the rest of it?"

Boris blinked, but his eyes just didn't want to stay open. Nearly drowning and having to drag oneself out of a surprisingly deep pool took a toll on a man.

Something poked him in the belly. Hard.

"Where's the rest of it?"

That sounded a bit like Igor, but it couldn't be. No squire would use such a tone to his master. Not unless he wanted to be clouted across the ear and assigned latrine duties for the next month. Two stints of latrine duty had surely taught Igor some manners by now.

And yet, whoever it was persisted to poke him most painfully.

Boris flung his arm out, shoving his tormentor away, before he forced his eyes open.

An angry Igor sat on the ground, presumably where he'd landed, with the dripping sceptre in his hands.

The sceptre Boris had been forced to leave in the pond, so that he might save himself from drowning.

"Give me that, boy," Boris said, stretching out his hand.

Igor stuck the sceptre behind his back. "No! You give me what you stole from the king, so I can take it back. You should have just taken the potion and run, or not drunk the ale, like I told you! Instead, you stole the crown jewels, so he knew you weren't dead, and he won't rest…I won't rest…until I bring back everything you stole, and you!" His voice had crept up higher in his panic, as though he knew he was on an impossible quest, but it was too late for him to refuse it.

Better for the boy to give up, head to some other kingdom, and find a less treacherous king to serve.

Boris rose. "He is no longer my king." He snatched the sceptre out of the boy's hands, and held it up high, where he could not reach it. "You can go back and tell him the only time he will see the crown jewels again is when he submits to justice for what he did. I will wear them to his execution."

Igor began jumping like a flea, trying to reach the sceptre. "You don't understand! I must bring them to him! I must!"

Boris sighed. "Then you're the stupidest squire who ever lived," he said sadly. With one swipe of his arm, he sent the boy sprawling, out cold.

He took the sceptre back the cave, where he packed it into the sack with all the other treasures. Then, he headed deeper into the forest, where Igor would not be able to find him. Even his stupid squire would have to give up some time.

Seventeen

When day dawned, it took but a moment for Rossa to get her bearings and remember where she was, before she threw open the shutters, to see the world outside. Not just one, but all the shutters, though at the first touch of chill air she put up a shield to keep the warmth inside the tower, while still letting her look out.

Sometime in the night, it had stopped snowing, and the sky was now as clear and crisp as the icicles that would soon festoon the eaves around the castle. The world…well, the world was white, smoothing the ground while it frosted the trees and shrubs, blanketing the roofs of cottage and monastery alike. Only the lake stood out, bright blue depths like a single, giant eye, staring at the sky above.

But it was the forest that drew her gaze, trees stretching endlessly up into the mountains for many miles more than she could see. She wouldn't be surprised if the forest did not thin until it reached the plains on the other side of the mountains, where the king's court lay. Not that she or any other sane person would travel that way, when there were roads and rivers, both far more sensible ways to reach the capital. If her father ever deemed her ready to go there.

He would. Maybe not this week or this month or even this year, given it was waning into winter, but he would.

As long as she did not slacken in her training. And what was a little snow, except a new challenge to be faced?

Movement caught her eye, between the trees, way down below. A creature of some kind…no, several of them. A herd of deer, she realised, fattened for winter but still searching for just a little more to eat before the final frosts set in.

She and Father had talked of going hunting, before he'd been summoned to Byzas. Because winter stews and sausages wouldn't be the same without a little smoked venison to season them. Without Father here, she'd have to go alone, but she didn't mind. She was more than a match for any deer.

She dressed for the hunt in clothes that had once been her brother's, though Tobias was much broader in the chest and shoulders now. Sure, the tunic was a little tight across her breasts, but it would do for today. Tomorrow, she could buy new ones in the village, at whatever tailor or weaver shops existed here in the mountains. Mother would approve of her bringing her trade to the local businesses, and they'd likely make warmer vestments than what was needed in Mirroten. They'd need the warmth up here in the mountains.

Maybe it was time to get a new winter cloak, too. She fancied a fur one, though she didn't think there was anything big enough in these mountains with the fur to fashion a whole cloak from. So pieces, maybe, from a hundred thieving squirrels…

Rossa laughed softly to herself. It would take all winter to amass so many squirrel pelts. Then again, it wasn't like she'd have anything else to do up here except hunt…

Venison first, then she could think about clothes, she scolded herself, taking her bow and a quiver of arrows, plus a brace of knives, as her weapons for today. A quick stop to the kitchen, where Sal plied her with fresh bread, a waterskin and some of the last autumn apples, and Rossa was soon headed out the gates, to the freedom of the high forests.

She mapped the forest in her mind's eye, trying to match what she'd seen from her tower to the view down here on the ground. The deer had been…that way, she decided, marching into the trees.

Her boots crunched through the snow, making her wish she'd chosen softer leather shoes instead. But they'd have been soaked in an instant, she knew, which was why she'd donned the heavy boots. Still, she was hardly a silent hunter, when anyone could hear her from miles away. Not even deer were that stupid.

If she intended to hunt today, she'd have to make it an ambush, lying in wait where no one would hear her. Of course, that meant guessing which way her prey would go, so that she might surprise them.

She cast her mind back to the view from the tower. Several streams meandered into the lake from the mountains, and the deer had been heading toward one. If she got there first and found a tree to hide in…her noisy boots would no longer matter.

Almost by magic, she found a fresh trail that led to the stream. Someone had tramped through the snow this way, breaking branches with the width of his shoulders, for she knew of no two-legged creature quite as destructive as an armoured man. Whoever he was, he would not hear her coming, for she took care to walk in his footsteps, where the squashed snow mixed with mud made little sound beneath her much lighter feet.

When she could hear the stream gurgling ahead, Rossa took to the trees, climbing the trunk of one before taking her boots off to use the branches as her barefoot highway. A whisper of magic added strength to branches that would not normally take her weight, as she slipped through to a gap in the trees.

There, she found a tiny waterfall, where the stream skipped down a line of rocks before tumbling into a pool a couple of yards below. The tree canopy here was so thick, no snow lay on the ground yet, though that would surely change as winter came. Instead, the pool's banks were carpeted in green.

Rossa wanted to laugh out loud. If she were a deer, whose food had been suddenly covered by snow, she'd be headed here, too. So she settled down to wait.

Sal's bread was half gone – Rossa hadn't dared risk crunching into an apple – when she finally spied movement. Down went the loaf, up went her bow, though she didn't reach for an arrow yet.

The buck entered the clearing first, ducking a little so his enormous rack of antlers didn't snag on the tree branches. Perhaps a dozen red deer followed him – a mix of does and juveniles. As they spread out along the stream, Rossa took her time assessing her options.

If she shot one of the smaller juveniles, she could probably dress the carcass and carry it home easily. But some of the juveniles came close to rivalling the buck for size, and the buck would be a prize for any hunter. She knew the buck's harem would winter just fine without him, likely finding another protector before the spring snow had melted. Still, she'd likely need to use magic to carry his carcass, for he was far too big for her. Then again, if she used her magic, she might be able to carry two home…

The obvious first choice was the juvenile who'd been at the back of the herd, a young male who'd be fighting for his own harem next year, if he lived that long. Bringing him down would likely panic the others, so she'd be lucky to get a second shot off, and she'd direct it toward the big buck.

She drew an arrow from her quiver, and sighted along it. The young male moved toward the trees, almost as if he sensed something wrong, before dropping his head to nibble at the grass once more. If she felled him just right, he'd block the trail, buying her time to take down the buck before they found another way out of the clearing.

A roar erupted, louder than any deer she'd ever heard. Who was the buck challenging?

Her target bolted, as the rest of the herd panicked.

To blazes with it. Rossa sent her arrow toward the antlered buck. It sank deep into the animal's eye, killing it, barely a moment before a massive paw broke the buck's neck.

Rossa reached for another arrow, aiming before she could truly process what she was seeing. It wasn't another deer that had roared, but a bear. A huge, white bear, which ripped her arrow out of the deer's eye and whirled to see where it had come from.

He spied her instantly, in her treetop perch. Her eyes met his, and she saw nothing but fury in them. Then he charged toward her.

Rossa didn't pause to think. She bolted.

Flying through the tree branches, leaping from one tree to another, until she reached the edge of the forest and was in sight of the castle gates. Still she ran, not stopping until she could bar the doors to the great hall and set her back against the impenetrable oak.

Sal came out of the kitchen to see what the noise was. She took in Rossa's dishevelled appearance and said, "Had a bit of a tumble, did you?"

Rossa shook her head, desperately trying to get enough breath in her lungs to force the words out. Finally, she managed to say, "There was a bear. In the forest."

Sal just smiled. "Oh, yes, we do get a few here. They come down from the mountains, to raid the orchards. They're quite partial to chestnuts and apples. They eat their fill and then go. Quite harmless, really, and nothing to fear, as long as you keep your distance and don't bother them. In spring, they sometimes bring the babies. Very cute to watch."

Rossa could only shake her head. There was nothing cute about that massive monster.

A monster she should have shot when she had the chance, she now realised, for a killer so huge, so close to the village was surely a danger to everyone here.

Instead, she'd run like a coward.

Anger fired her blood. Not at the bear, but at herself. How could she be so stupid?

"I'll be in the yard, chopping wood," Rossa managed to say, her hands shaking as she unbarred the door. She peered around the yard cautiously, making sure the bear hadn't followed her, before she dashed toward the axe and the chopping block.

If the bear did come here, this time, she'd be prepared.

Eighteen

Boris eyed the buck. The beast would be his dinner tonight, and perhaps on the morrow, too.

In the past, he might have brought it down with a well-placed arrow, but he hadn't thought to bring a bow when he left the capital, so he made do with what weapons he had. He leaped from his hiding place, fastening both arms around the beast's neck, and then he twisted until the bones snapped. Only then did he let the buck fall to the ground.

Boris blinked. There was an arrow in the

buck's eye. An arrow that had certainly not been there a moment before.

He had no arrows, nor a bow, which meant…

Igor had found him again.

Boris scanned the trees, searching for his accursed squire. There, a flash of colour where it did not belong, and a terrified eye peering through the leaves. Boris roared in fury, and raced across the clearing.

The boy, more monkey than man, fled through the branches, faster than Boris could follow.

Boris sighed. He did not understand why the boy didn't just give up. After all, Boris let him go, much as he'd allowed the remaining Bisseni to flee into the mountains when the battle was done. Some things just weren't worth pursuing.

That deer, however, wasn't something he wanted to lose. He butchered it as best he could, and carried it back to his cave. Somewhere along the way, he'd acquired a flint and tinder, and while he knew he could eat the venison raw, he much preferred his meat cooked, which he could manage over the small fire he kept burning.

What he'd give to taste a proper hunter's stew, laced with pork and venison…one day, he promised himself. When he'd finally dissuaded the squire from hunting him.

Nineteen

It was a full week – and a month's worth of chopped firewood – before Rossa could bring herself to enter the forest again. Plenty of people who remembered her from when she was small had come to reassure her about the bears in the woods. They'd all advised her to bring a bag of apples with her if she went into the forest again, for all the local bears would completely ignore her for a bag of apples.

When she tried to explain what she'd seen, no one believed her. The bear had only looked so big because she was frightened, they'd said.

They preferred fruit to meat, though they occasionally ate carrion if they were starving at the end of a long winter. It must have been a very light brown, not white…

And so it went, on and on, until even Rossa was inclined to misbelieve her own senses.

But she knew she had seen the white monster bear kill a stag. The deer herd had panicked at the sight of it, too, so they'd known how dangerous it was.

Therefore, she had little choice but to venture into the forest, kill the monster, and bring back its body as proof. Then, she might persuade someone in the village to turn the beast's hide into a warm winter cloak that she intended to wear everywhere.

Even Father would have to take notice if she killed a monster. After all, wasn't that what his job entailed?

Today, she carried her bow and a new quiver of arrows – the old one was lost in the forest somewhere – twice as many daggers as before, and she'd found a leather breastplate with a matching helm in the armoury that seemed about her size. Likely they'd belonged to the squire of a crusading knight, centuries ago, but they were hers now. Sure, she could conjure a magical shield, but it didn't hurt to have a little mundane protection, too. Especially when she'd seen how easily the bear had broken the buck's neck.

She sent out a finding spell, the sort of thing Swanhild excelled at, and was not surprised to find the bear near the same clearing.

Of course he was.

There'd been no new snowfall, so what was left sat in patches beside the muddy trail, sometimes humped so high she'd wondered if what she saw was the bear, lying in wait.

But she didn't see him at all.

When she reached the clearing, she debated whether to walk right in, or climb a tree again. Then she cursed herself for a simpleton and scaled the nearest tree. She hoped her father never heard of her moment of stupidity. She was lucky it hadn't cost her her life.

Today, the clearing was empty, much as it had been a week ago. Though there should be some sign of what had happened. The buck's body, or at least what remained of it.

Yet…there was nothing, not even any visible blood.

Her quiver sat in the tree she'd watched from before, leaning against the tree trunk like it was waiting for her. Cursing softly under her breath, Rossa wove her way through the branches to it. Better to have two quivers of arrows than one, especially when she still hadn't spotted the bear. She scanned the clearing, then turned to peer between the trees behind her, as well. Every snowdrift might be the bear hiding, plotting an ambush.

She snorted softly. Bears did not plot ambushes. They were creatures of instinct, without the kind of foresight and planning a man might possess. All a bear thought about was food and fighting and…ah, mating. She felt the heat rise in her cheeks. There were men back in Mirroten just like that, including her young nephew, Bruno.

Something moved in the snow. No…sparkled, as it caught the sunlight, filtering through the leaves, before the shaft of light vanished, then returned again.

Rossa moved closer, shifting from tree to

tree until she stood over the object. It appeared to be a large brooch, with a dark stone that glittered red in the sun. It looked like one of the treasures Father brought home for Mother, when he came home from a mission. Except Rossa knew every item in Mother's jewellery chest, and this wasn't one of them.

She dropped from the tree to the ground, and reached for the brooch. The moment her fingers closed around it, the ground dropped out from under her. Rossa opened her mouth to scream, but then her head collided with something, and the world went dark.

Twenty

Boris peered into the pit trap, searching for the brooch he'd used as bait to lure Igor in. Blasted boy, he'd managed to drag it into the hole with him. Thankfully, Boris was much taller than the boy, so he hooked his legs around the nearest tree and lowered himself over the lip of the hole. He'd have to move Igor's unconscious body to the side to get to it, though.

Boris rolled the boy onto his side…only to find it wasn't Igor at all, but some girl he'd never seen before.

He'd caught an innocent in his trap. Worse, she was bleeding from the blow to the head that had knocked her out.

Only one thing to do, then. Boris climbed down into the hole, grabbed the brooch and the girl, then laid them on the lip before hauling himself out, too.

What to do with her? He could hardly take her to the nearest healer – he had no idea who or where they might be, even if the healer didn't faint in terror at the sight of him.

He should take her to his cave, lay her down beside the fire, and wait for her to wake up.

And what if she didn't? He'd seen men take head wounds in war, from which they never recovered. Never woke…

No, she would wake, beside his fire, and he'd make sure she got home safely.

Somehow without letting her see him.

Boris sighed. What were her family thinking, letting this slip of a girl wander alone in the woods?

Twenty-One

The ghost of a headache haunted Rossa when she woke, stiff from a longer sleep than she would have liked on a bed that was most certainly not her own. Heavens above, had she fallen asleep in that hole?

No, she'd been knocked out, which is why her head still hurt, she told herself, touching the amulet she wore under her clothes at all times. She must have been bleeding, which activated the amulet's healing powers while she was unconscious. It must have been bad to still hurt, even a little, after so long.

She sat up, scanning her surroundings. A fire burned to her left, and stone walls – formed, not made – curved around her. She'd fallen into a cave, then, she mused, glancing up to see how far she'd fallen. Yet the stone stretched above her, too, smooth except for the spiky teeth she'd seen hang from cave ceilings in some of Father's books.

She hadn't fallen here, she'd been carried, and someone had lit that fire.

She wasn't alone. She reached out with her magic, sensing a second heartbeat in the cave with her, hidden in the shadows, deeper inside.

"Come out," she ordered. "I know you're there. There's no point hiding."

Whoever it was had not taken her knives from her, and her bow lay on the ground within easy reach, along with her quivers. Either he was so strong he didn't fear her, weapons or no, or he was stupid.

Whoever he was, she was going to make him regret trapping her and then kidnapping her. By the time she was done with him, there would be nothing left for her father to cut off. Killing him would be a mercy.

Something moved in the dark, shuffling against the stone, but no one appeared.

"I'm going to count to three, and if you don't come out on your own, I'm going to light this cave up as bright as day, and then I'm coming in after you to drag you out." Rossa took a deep breath. "All right. One…two…"

Still he stayed in the dark. The man who'd made the path to the clearing, trudging through the snow, she decided, remembering the broken branches along the way. The size of his boot prints. He was huge, a giant even, but her magic was more than a match for any man, no matter how big.

"Three," she finished, and conjured a ball of light that she threw at him.

It splashed against the wall behind him, outlining him in blazing white for a moment before the magic sputtered out.

Rossa let out the breath she hadn't even realised she was holding. She was in a cave with…the bear.

Who was now moving toward her, stepping out of the shadows and into the flickering firelight. On two legs, like a man.

No, he was a bear, not a man.

"Where is your master? The man who brought me here?" she asked.

The bear shook his head.

"You don't know, or you can't tell me?" she pressed.

The bear stared at her, something like frustration burning in his eyes. Slowly, he brought a mighty paw up to his chest, over where his heart might be. Then he bowed, the way her father did to her mother.

"If you were a man, I'd imagine you mean to say something like, 'I am Sir Pompous Arse of Dead Deer Pond, at your service, my lady.'"

The bear made a strange sound in his throat, while his eyes appeared to crinkle.

"Yeah, I wouldn't like being called Sir Pompous Arse, either. Snow White the Bear, then, until you tell me otherwise." Rossa rose to her feet and dropped a sort of curtsy, spreading the edges of her cloak in place of a skirt. "Lady Rossa of Mirroten. But you can call me Rossa. Everyone else does. Well, if you could, I mean."

She shook her head, which gave a twinge to

remind her that she'd been hurt. "Look at me, talking to a bear. The monster bear which took down my deer a week ago. I know I hit my head but…"

The bear leaned down, picked something up off the ground, and held it out to her. It was the brooch.

Rossa sighed. "Yeah, if I'm going to dream up crazy things, of course I'd include jewellery worth a king's ransom. I don't know what things are like among bears, but you can't just give something so costly to a girl you barely know. Is it even yours?"

The bear touched its head, at almost the same spot where hers hurt most. Then it held the brooch out again, insistence in its eyes.

"Fine, I'll take it. In payment for the bump on the head, and for stealing my deer. That was my kill, not yours. It was already dead when you broke its neck."

If bears had eyebrows, his would have risen. Maybe he did have eyebrows, as white as the rest of his fur, and she just couldn't see them. He pointed at the antlers lying in the corner of the cave, then at her.

Antlers, but no other part of the deer. As if he'd butchered the carcass and buried it, like a man might.

"I suppose for someone the size of you, a whole deer wouldn't last you more than a week," Rossa said. A memory pricked at her mind, and she searched through her things until she found the sack Sal had given her. "Here, I brought you some apples. The castle cook, who is also the innkeeper in the village, said I should give them to you." Honesty made her add, "Actually, she said I should give them to you to distract you, so I could get away."

Surprise widened his eyes, before the bear bowed again, gesturing toward the cave entrance.

"If I didn't know better, I'd think you're telling me I'm free to go," Rossa said, eyeing the bear as her hand closed around the knife at her hip.

The bear inclined his head. Almost…regally.

She dropped the sack of apples at his feet. "Well, enjoy them. There's plenty more back home, though I suspect if I'm not quick, someone will turn them into cider. Maybe I should ask the cook to set aside a barrel or two, so I can bring you some, if I come to visit you again." She'd definitely hit her head, if she was talking about paying visits to bears. "Nice to meet you, I guess."

Her shoulders itched as she turned her back on the bear, and forced herself to stroll out of the cave, across the clearing, and all the way back to the castle, without pausing to look back.

Twenty-Two

Boris followed the girl through the forest, surprised to find the village – and the castle where she was headed – weren't at all far from his cave. Perhaps it wasn't so strange her family allowed her to wander through the woods, when she was so close to home.

She'd slipped the brooch into her pocket on her way home. Boris had wondered whether she'd wear it or sell it, until he saw the guards bow to her when she entered the castle. He'd known then that she wouldn't sell it, though he still wasn't sure whether she'd wear such a jewel. She lived in such an isolated castle, wearing men's clothes, instead of the silk gowns seen in court that befitted such a brooch.

Then, of course, he wondered what she'd look like in a wine-coloured gown, her dark curls tamed only by a crown of such splendour it cast the brooch into the shade…

In fact, he was certain he'd seen just such a crown in the sack he'd taken from the capital, encrusted with so many diamonds and rubies, you could scarcely see the silver metal beneath. So valuable it had been kept under lock and key in the capital, only being brought out to wear on the most momentous occasions.

Hardly the sort of thing you gave to a girl chance met in the woods. Then again, that brooch wasn't, either, and he'd handed it to her without a thought.

Silly bear with silly ideas. What had he been thinking?

He hadn't been thinking, which was the problem.

After swearing he would watch from the shadows, where she wouldn't see him when she woke, he'd definitely made a mess of things. Then again, he'd expected her to feel fear at the sight of him, and there'd been none whatsoever.

Ah, but she'd fired the arrow at the buck that day, hadn't she? It hadn't been Igor shooting at him at all.

A very strange girl, this Lady…Rose, is that what she'd said her name was? Whose eyes had glowed as red as the ruby brooch in the sun when she'd cast the spell which lit up the cave.

She was a witch, then, with powers beyond those of normal men. Boris had heard of such women, but he'd never met one, and he could not deny she intrigued him. For a slip of a girl to feel no fear in the presence of a monstrous bear, when she'd seen him kill…she must be a powerful witch indeed.

Perhaps she could break the spell that had made him into a bear. Or, failing that, cast some sort of enchantment that would keep Igor away from him, and help him find his way back to court, where he would see Sviatopolk pay for his crimes.

If only he could ask her.

Twenty-Three

Rossa tossed and turned all night, debating what to do about the white bear. A day earlier, she'd been certain she should kill him, but now she wasn't sure. He'd pulled her out of that trap, lit a fire, buried a deer, bowed, given her a priceless gift, and maybe even laughed…in every respect, more like a man than a bear.

None of the villagers had seen him – they spoke only of brown bears, maybe as big as a man, and not a white one who stood head and shoulders above any man she'd ever met. Certainly not one who hunted deer.

No one from the village had mysteriously gone missing, either, or in such a way that the bear might be blamed.

That didn't mean anything, though. He might have only recently arrived in the area, so that he hadn't had the time to pose a danger to the village.

For a bear who could master fire was very dangerous indeed…

Which was why, as the first streaks of dawn lightened the sky, she stood at the mouth of the cave she'd woken up in yesterday. Inside, the bear was snoring beside a campfire that had burned down to glowing coals.

If he was a danger to her mother's people, she should slaughter him and be done with it. Yet even now she hesitated.

Was he a man or a beast?

She sent a whisper of magic through him, searching for the answer. He was a magical beast, with the heart and soul of the man he'd once been before someone had cast a spell on him. The magic was not his own, for if it were, it would course through his blood as it did hers, yet it was still a part of him, bonded to his bones, somehow. It was no mere enchantment or glamour, to be dispelled with a wave of her hand. No, to remove this spell might kill him.

While she'd been lost in thought, the snoring had stopped. The bear was awake.

Yet he did not move to attack her, and she did him the same courtesy.

"Did you want to be turned into a bear?" she said.

The bear sat up, then shook his head.

"Do you wish you were a man again?" she persisted.

The bear cocked his head to the side, thoughtful. As if he didn't have a ready answer to give her without words.

"Do you know if there is a way to break the curse? Did the witch tell you how you might become a man again?"

Another shake of his head.

Perhaps it was not possible. But animal transformations were usually curses, punishments for offending a witch in some way. It was dangerous to cast a curse that could not be broken. Usually the caster had to pay a high price, in her own blood, for her negligence. So either the witch had been playing a dangerous game…or the spell upon the bear was a blessing, not a curse, even if he had not asked for it.

"Did this…did this happen to you because someone was trying to help you?" Rossa asked.

His eyes regarded her, filled with yearning. Yearning for the words a bear could not say.

"Do you know the witch who did this to you?"

He shook his head.

Wonderful. So some witch had likely cast a spell on him as he slept. She was lucky he hadn't attacked her for waking him.

Rossa perched on a rock just inside the cave. "So now you're stuck as a bear, with no way of going back to the way you were."

He inclined his head.

She kept her eyes firmly fixed on his as she drawled, "Well, that's quite the problem, Snow. But I have a bigger one. Because I need to know if you're a danger to the people who live around here. My mother's people, in the village, and the monastery, and the castle. Are you going to hurt them, Snow?" With deliberate care, she conjured a fireball in her hand. The sort that gave off smoke and heat and definitely did damage when she threw it at someone. "Are you my enemy, Snow?"

His gaze never left hers as he shook his head slowly.

"Good." She turned the fireball into a ball of pure magic, then threw it at him.

When the ball hit his chest, it exploded into a shower of sparkles. He blinked, then raised those eye ridges that definitely supported his invisible eyebrows.

"If you meant to harm me, that spell would not have shattered harmlessly against you," she said.

He snorted, then held up his enormous paws, claws extended.

Rossa waved her hand, and a small shield encased his paws, so he could no longer move them. "Size doesn't matter as much when it comes to magic. My little magic hands are more than a match for your extra large ones, any day."

His eyes crinkled, just as they had yesterday,

and the same sound came from his throat.

Laughter, Rossa realised.

Not the response she was used to. Her father would have given her one of his opaque looks, and told her that skill or quickness of mind mattered far more than size or power, before telling her to repeat the training exercise.

She pulled out the sack of food she'd taken from the kitchen. Bread, meat, cheese, fruit — even a handful of dried chestnuts that had been soaking in warm water overnight, and were now tender enough to eat.

"I'll need to get back to my training when it's light enough to see, but my father says the best warriors are ones who are well-fed. So, would you like to break your fast with me, Snow?"

The bear inclined his head, and for the first time in her life, Rossa found herself sharing a meal with a bear. The first of many, as it would turn out.

Twenty-Four

Boris began to look forward to Rose's visits, and not just because she brought him food. She wore boys' clothes because she came into the forest to train to fight and hunt, both of which she was particularly skilled at. She reminded him a little of the Bisseni raiders who could appear out of nowhere, attack, then melt into the mountains as if they'd never existed, except she left little trace of her presence.

More than once, he'd caught himself comparing her to Vica.

If Vica had been able to fight, and defend herself like Rose did, she might still be alive.

No, if he'd been a better protector and husband, Vica would never have needed to fight, and she'd still be alive, he corrected himself.

Vica would not have been able to wear a boy's tunic and hose, especially not after Lida was born. The tunic would have been too tight across her breasts, and the hose were too narrow for her generous hips.

Which was why comparisons between the two women were silly. Vica had been a wife and mother, while Rose was only a girl, unmarried without the responsibilities of running a household, even if she was the same age as Vica had been when she died.

And Rose was…unique, he decided, leaning back to watch her.

Now the snow lay thick on the ground, she'd put it to use, crafting little snowmen that she brought to life with magic. She'd made them dance like children's puppets at first, making him laugh, until she'd turned serious. Now the little figures darted around the clearing like angry demons while she hunted them. First with magic, then with real blades, thrown with such deadly accuracy that if they had been demons, they'd have been slaughtered for sure. Because they were her magical pets, though, the dismembered snowmen barely paused before the pieces got up and rejoined the hunt as smaller, more numerous targets.

She whirled and spun, leaped and shot, never missing, with an intensity of focus Boris had only seen in his best warriors. He began to wonder if he'd be any match for her in close combat. She was so fast…

Finally, Rose stopped to catch her breath, shooting a beaming smile that stabbed straight to his heart. God, she was beautiful.

"I need to spar with someone. Were you any good in the practice yard, Snow? We'll pick a spot where there's plenty of snow to cushion your fall, and I'll try not to hurt you." Rose sheathed her daggers, then beckoned. "Come on, fight me."

Boris looked her up and down – he was more than twice her size! One swipe of his paw and he'd send her flying.

She seemed to be able to read his mind. "I'm not stupid, Snow. Any man I fight is likely to be bigger than me. Confident in his size and strength. It doesn't matter. I need to be able to beat him."

Reluctantly, he lurched to his feet and took up a fighting stance. His hands itched to hold a sword again, but he knew his claws were deadly enough. Worse, he could not retract them, so each of his fingers was tipped with a wickedly curved dagger that could slice her open.

"Ready?" she asked.

He couldn't hit a woman. Not even this girl, with both her hands up and curled into fists, like she wanted to punch him.

Nevertheless, he nodded.

Her hands never moved, but somehow, her body twisted, and a blow to his gut knocked all the air out of his lungs. A second blow sent him face-first into a snowdrift.

"Snow? Are you all right?"

The gentle caress of her magic lifted him back onto his feet.

"Did I hurt you? Have you never fought before?" she asked, her eyes wide with concern.

Boris shook his head. The only part of him that she'd hurt was his pride, and heaven knew he had pride to spare. Cautiously, he mirrored her fighting stance, then inclined his head to tell her he was ready.

A moment later, when he came up, spitting out a fresh mouthful of snow, he knew he had not been ready at all.

A lifetime of war might not be enough to defend against the whirlwind that was Rose.

And yet…if the only good thing that came out of all this was that he helped one woman to fight, to not fall victim as Vica had, then Boris would know that his life had not been wasted. That Vica had not died in vain, and might even be smiling on him now.

Well, hopefully not now, with him arse-up in the snow and all.

He clambered to his feet, once more taking his stance.

This time, he would…

Wham.

…not drown in the icy pond.

Boris came up, gasping, then clawed his way over the bank and out of the water.

Rose looked worried. "I think that's enough fighting for today. I brought a jar of mulled wine and left it by the fire. It should be warm by now, and I think you need a hot drink in you after that dunking. Whoever you were before you became a bear, Snow, I don't think you were a warrior."

He wished he could argue, but her arm around his middle as she tried to help him inside sent a warm tingle through him that went straight to his heart.

And…maybe other parts, too.

Yes, a cup or two of mulled wine would likely send him straight to sleep, where he might dream of her, and what they might do, what he might tell her, if he was a man and not this clumsy beast. A dream that would make even a bear blush.

Twenty-Five

A particularly fat flock of pigeons had been found in the barn, gorging on the wheat waiting to be milled into flour. One of the miller's boys chased them off, while his brothers boarded up the barn so that they could not get in again, but not before Rossa had seen the fat birds in flight.

Pigeons roasted nicely over a fire, especially fat ones. She'd seen thieves hanged for stealing a bag of precious wheat, where most people could only afford chestnut flour for their bread. So a death sentence for the pigeons seemed fitting.

She set out into the forest to hunt them, hoping to find their roost, if not the pigeons themselves. If she could catch a couple, though, she might share them with Snow, for surely the bear hadn't eaten a fresh roasted pigeon in quite some time.

With a little help from her magic, she soon found where they'd flow off to, for the stupid birds had perched all together. Perhaps they were too fat to fly far.

Rossa strung her bow, nocked an arrow to the string, then selected her target – a particularly plump bird perched on a branch lower than the others.

She drew the arrow back, sighted along it, blew out a breath and…

The whole flock whirred into flight.

Cursing, Rossa fired at the nearest bird. It might not be the choicest, but she was damned if she was leaving here empty handed.

A squawk told her she'd hit her target, before it whumped heavily to earth.

Yet when the cloud of feathers cleared, she was surprised to see she'd hit a boy, not a bird at all. He must have climbed the tree to try and catch a bird, and he'd fallen out when she shot him. The arrow stuck out of his side, where it might have missed most of his important organs, but he'd bleed plenty if she tried to pull it out.

She'd need to find some yarrow to staunch the bleeding first, then.

Luckily, he'd knocked himself out in his fall from the tree, so he was likely going to lie there while she found what she needed.

Thanking Swanhild for teaching her this particular spell, she searched the forest for the nearest patch of yarrow. It wasn't far off, but it did involve some scrambling over rocks to reach it. Plucking handfuls of the feathery leaves that she then stuffed into a pocket in her cloak, she headed back to the injured boy.

The innocent she'd shot.

If her father knew…

Grimly, she pressed her lips together and knelt beside the unconscious boy. His tunic was so thin and threadbare, it was a wonder he hadn't frozen to death out here. Even his cloak had more holes than cloth. Whoever he was,

he could not have come from the village –
Mother and the monastery would never have
allowed one of their neighbours to live in such
poverty. Perhaps he was a pilgrim, who'd
gotten lost on the way to the monastery.

Whatever or whoever he was, she'd take
him there once she'd finished healing him.

She lifted the hem of his tunic, pulling it up
carefully so as not to disturb the arrow. He was
painfully thin, this strange boy, his ribs sharply
outlined beneath his skin. Definitely not from
the village, where no one would be allowed to
starve.

She took a deep breath when she reached
the arrowhead, then peeled the cloth away
from his skin with the utmost care. To her
surprise, the arrow came away with the cloth,
revealing no wound beneath.

She yanked the arrow out of his tunic,
finding it had gone straight through both the
front and back of the fabric. How it had
missed him, she did not know. It should have
grazed him, at the least, but there was no sign
of blood or a wound on his body, and the dark
brown of his tunic hid any bloodstains that

might have been absorbed by the cloth.

Rossa sat back on her heels, not sure what to do. She should carry the unconscious boy back to town, where he might get a good meal and some clothes he wouldn't freeze to death in.

The boy chose that moment to wake up, his eyes growing wide as he scrambled backwards, away from her.

"You shot me!" he accused.

"I was shooting at the pigeons," Rossa hedged. "I must have missed and hit your tunic instead."

The boy looked down, and his eyes grew wider still. He stuck two fingers through the hole in his tunic and made an obscene gesture through it. "You tore a hole right through it! My last good shirt! You…stupid peasant! Can't even tell the difference between a pigeon and a person!"

Rossa almost laughed. If anyone was a peasant, it was this boy, in his rough rags. "Come back to the village with me, and I'll see that you get a new shirt," she offered. It was the least she could do.

He reared back in horror, his face curling with disdain that would not have looked out of place on Bruno's face. "Certainly not! I'm not going anywhere with a peasant girl who shoots people!"

He stood up, dusted himself off, and marched away into the forest. In the opposite direction to the village.

Rossa just shook her head. She could use magic to bring the boy back with her, but why bother with such a rude wretch? If he didn't want her help, he could go off and freeze in the forest, if that's what he wished.

Meanwhile, she'd have to go back to the castle to fetch some food to take to Snow, instead of the fresh pigeon she'd hoped to catch. Or go deeper into the forest in her pursuit of those thieving pigeons.

Sighing, Rossa set off.

Twenty-Six

The first day Rose didn't visit him, Boris wasn't worried. Something at the castle must have kept her, he told himself. While she might not be the lady of these lands – that title belonged to her mother, he'd come to understand – she would still have some responsibilities, even if she ran away from them and into the forest most days.

She would come to visit him when she could.

But then he almost ran into Igor on one of the game trails, managing to hide just in time.

Yes, it was definitely his traitorous squire and not Rose in boys' garb. Boris did his best to avoid the boy, and not lead him to the cave where he kept the sack of jewels, but everywhere he went, the boy seemed to appear.

Why wouldn't the former squire leave him alone?

Fuming, Boris set a trap for the boy – a pit trap, like the one Rose had fallen into. He baited it with a particularly ugly jewel fashioned out of gold so blackened with age it no longer glittered like it was supposed to. Igor coveted this particular piece as much as any of the prettier ones, but it would not draw the eye of anyone else.

It didn't even draw Igor's eye for several days, during which Rose was conspicuously absent. Had Igor somehow driven her away?

Perhaps the boy had attacked her, and fear had kept her at home.

No. Rose the Red, powerful witch that she was, feared nothing and no one. If she didn't fear him, she definitely wouldn't be frightened by a boy smaller than she was.

Unless he'd somehow surprised her, and she was hurt…

Boris's heart constricted in his chest at the thought of her lying unconscious and wounded, as

she had by his fire that first day they'd met.

If Igor had hurt her, he'd kill the boy.

A shout, followed by the thump of something falling, told him his trap had finally ensnared the boy.

The trap would hold him while Boris went up to the castle to see if Rose was all right.

He had only to see her, to know she was safe, and he could return.

If she was injured…

Then the boy would be right here, stuck in the trap, to answer for his crimes.

Boris nodded, then headed up to the village.

Twenty-Seven

Rossa was in the practice yard, taking aim at the archery target, when the screams started. She was supposed to be in the kitchen, helping Sal prepare tomorrow's Yule feast, when the whole town would come to the great hall to celebrate Christmas, but after she'd managed to tip a whole pot of honey on the flagstones instead of on the roast boar, and set one of the puddings on fire…Sal had shooed her out, saying she had hands enough to help her with the feast preparations. Sal said she'd call her if she needed her, so not to go far.

Rossa had sighed, knowing there would be no such call. She'd promised Mother she'd stay until the end of the feast, for it was rare enough that they came to the castle, and her people needed to see her. To know she shared their celebration and their sorrows, as well as the bounty of her table.

Rossa hoped Sal didn't tell Mother she'd almost set the table on fire, too.

But that meant she was stuck in the castle grounds, unable to head into the forest to spend the day with Snow, or even continue her hunt for those pilfering pigeons.

Those bloody pigeons…

It was almost as bad as being stuck in a scarlet wool gown that swished everywhere she went. So much for being a silent hunter on swift feet.

But she could still shoot, and while her skirts might impede her movement, they were no obstacle to her magic, so when she heard screams coming from the bailey, she brought her bow and arrows with her.

So that she might aim them at…

She blinked.

Maids ran screaming, for with no guards at the gate, now the mountain passes were closed and no one could enter or leave the town from outside, he'd wandered straight in, with no one to stop him.

"Shoot it!" one of the maids shrieked as she ran past Rossa into the castle proper.

But Rossa could not even bring herself to lift her bow.

"Snow?" she asked uncertainly. Surely there could not be more than one monstrous white bear in the mountains, but with the maids screaming so... "What are you doing here?"

The bear turned – for he stood on his hind legs, taller than any man – and stared at her. Then he lifted one enormous paw and pointed at her.

"It's Christmas, Snow. I can't go into the woods today. I'm needed here," she said, knowing even as the words left her lips that they were a lie. She wasn't needed, here or anywhere. For all that this was her family's castle, she had no place here. In the forest, it was different, but here...

Snow inclined his head, as if he understood.

Then he bowed deeply, making her wonder if he truly had been a knight before he'd been transformed, and turned to go.

Her heart twisted within her, somehow wringing what moisture there was in her mouth until it was almost too dry to speak. Yet she could not bear to see him go, not when he'd come here to see her. It was Yule, and he was here, and the one person she wanted to see most of anyone. "Come inside, Snow. I haven't had my midday meal yet. I'm sure there's food enough in the kitchens for us to share."

She crossed the bailey, then threw open the doors to the great hall. Gritting her teeth, she took the folds of her skirt in both hands and performed her best curtsy, the sort her Father insisted she know in case she ever had to go to court and meet royalty.

Snow inclined his head, the way she imagined a king might, and went inside.

Twenty-Eight

The hall was set up for a feast, with all the tables and benches set out in readiness for guests who were not yet here.

Rose seemed to be able to read his thoughts, for she said, "We are hosting a Christmas feast tomorrow. The whole village is invited, including the monks. It is Mother's gift to her people. It's empty now because everyone is in the kitchens. Well, except me, because…I can't cook." She tucked her hands into the folds of her voluminous skirts and stared at the floor, as if ashamed to admit she had shortcomings.

He wished he could tell her that it didn't matter whether a lady could cook, for it was her husband's job to provide servants for her, if that's what she wanted.

She took off her cloak, hanging it on a peg beside the massive fireplace. And then she turned around.

Boris couldn't take his eyes off her. All these weeks, he'd seen her in her hunting clothes, bundled up against the winter cold in shapeless tunics that hid everything, but the gown she wore today…made it hard to draw breath.

It was modest enough, leaving nothing but her face and hands bare as the skirt swept dangerously close to the floor, but the cloth clung to her as ardently as a lover. Caressing her breasts, curving around her hips, all the while highlighting her delicate blush under his scrutiny, her lips ruddy from being bitten…she was Rose the Red incarnate today, both as delicate and as brazen as a rose in full bloom.

If only he were a man and not a bear…

Rose cleared her throat. "I'll just head down to the kitchen for some food. You should…probably stay here, out of sight, so you don't scare anyone else. Maybe…warm yourself by the fire?"

At home, any fireplace this large would have hunting dogs lolling about in front of it. Yet here, he had the space to himself. One reason to prefer being a bear to a man was that he might stretch out before the hearth, without worrying about dignity, or whether he'd get soot on his clothes.

So he accepted Rose's invitation, and luxuriated in the warmth from a blaze much bigger than the tiny campfires he kept burning in his cave.

Until the imperious tap of footsteps that did not belong to Rose's hunter-trained feet entered the room. The woman who owned the footsteps, the feet and undoubtedly every stone in the floor beneath them made an irritable noise in her throat.

Boris raised his head to meet her gaze.

Ah, so this was the lady of the castle, Rose's mother. Though her hair was almost all white to Rose's dark curls, and wrinkles blurred the beauty that he didn't doubt had once rivalled

Rose's own, the resemblance was too close to ignore.

Boris rose to his full height, before offering the lady his best courtly bow, as befit a guest accepting her generous hospitality.

If she chose to offer it. From the frown on her face, he wasn't sure whether she wanted to turn him out or summon guards to slaughter him.

"Rossa!" she called, her tone promising dire consequences if her daughter didn't appear immediately.

Rose…no, Rossa, he corrected himself…raced up the steps and bobbed a quick curtsy. "Yes, Mother?"

The woman stabbed a finger in Boris's direction. "The servants tell me you brought a bear into the house. Is that your bear?"

Rossa hunched her shoulders. "Um…yes? And no? He's…he's sort of his own bear. I brought him in here, but…"

"He bowed to me." She made it sound like a crime.

Rossa wrung her hands. "He's…well, he's not really a bear. All right, he is a bear, but…"

She buried her face in her hands for moment, then met her mother's gaze again. She sighed. "Snow, this is my mother, Lady Sara of Mirroten, and we're in her home."

Boris bowed once more. Crime or not, it was the courteous thing to do.

"And Mother, this is…well, I don't know his real name, as bears can't really talk, but I call him Snow White, because his fur's white, and…he didn't like the other name I tried to call him."

What had that been? Oh, she'd called him Sir Pompous Arse when they'd first met. Boris much preferred Snow.

One sharp nod was all the acknowledgement he got from Lady Sara.

"Why is he here?"

Rossa stared at her feet. "He's…he came to see me, and I invited him to dinner, because we usually share dinner when I'm in the woods, and because I have to stay here, I wanted…"

Understanding softened Lady Sara's gaze, though Rossa didn't see it. "Is he dangerous?" Lady Sara asked.

Boris bowed his head. Yes, he was.

When Rossa didn't answer, Sara added, "I mean, is he a danger to anyone here? Will he hurt the villagers, or the servants?"

No mention of Rossa or herself. Interesting. Did that mean Sara was a witch, too, as powerful as her daughter?

Sara continued, "I'm sure I don't need to remind you, but you are Lady Rossa, and you have a duty to protect your people as much as I do. So if this bear is a danger to them, a bear you brought into the castle among them, then it will be your responsibility to drive him out, or otherwise remove the danger to protect your people."

Rossa stared at him, anguish in her eyes. "I can't kill Snow, Mother. He won't harm anyone here – will you give your word, Snow? Please?"

If he'd been able to speak, Boris would have offered them both his heartfelt promise to respect the laws of hospitality, in thanks for allowing him into their home. Instead, he placed a hand on his heart and dropped to one knee, bowing his head.

Lady Sara's mouth twitched, almost as if she were trying to hide a smile. "I've seen many things in my life, but that's the first time I've ever seen a bear swear fealty to someone, let alone me. Fine, your magic bear can stay for one night, as long as he confines himself to the great hall, but he must be gone in the morning. With the whole village coming for the feast…he cannot stay any longer than that. And as he's your guest, you'll have to come up with a Yule gift for him. I have enough to do." She marched off.

Rossa blew out a relieved breath. "I can't believe she let you stay. If my father were here, he would not have permitted it."

Boris nodded. He would have killed a bear that came within ten yards of Vica or Lida.

"Especially if he found out you were once a knight. Father does not like knights," Rossa explained.

What manner of man did not like knights? They fought for the king, or their liege lord, and as Rossa's father and Lady Sara's husband, the man was surely a nobleman himself.

"Don't worry about Father. He's…off doing

something for the Emperor. He won't be home before spring," Rossa said, patting his arm. "Now, the food should be ready, so I'll just go down to the kitchen to fetch it, because none of the maids will dare come in here while there's a bear in the hall."

And again she departed, but this time Boris took a seat at one of the tables. He might have the strength and appearance of a bear, but he had the heart and soul of a prince, and he owed these ladies his best behaviour.

And a Yule gift, he realised, his heart sinking. That would present a problem.

Twenty-Nine

Even after spending half the night in the great hall with Snow, talking and drinking far more mead than was good for her, Rossa woke at dawn. Only to discover she'd never left the great hall – she'd slept on the hearth, wrapped in her cloak and a blanket someone must have brought from somewhere.

But Snow…was nowhere to be seen.

She raced outside, hoping to catch him before he departed, but the bailey was empty. Cursing, she headed back inside for some warmer clothes, so she might follow him back to the forest.

Only to run into Mother at the bottom of the stairs. Whose grave gaze told her she wasn't going anywhere until the feast was over.

"Is your magical bear gone?" Mother asked.

He wasn't hers. He was…tears threatened to spill from her eyes. Tears Rossa blinked ruthlessly away as she nodded, not trusting her voice.

"He left you a gift."

It took Rossa a moment before she followed her mother's pointing finger to the table where they'd eaten dinner yesterday. The plates, cups and jugs were gone, replaced by four fat fish, each as long as her arm, arranged in a square on the tabletop. All bearing the unmistakeable marks of a bear's claws about their gills.

He'd hooked them out of the water with his bare hands, Rossa realised.

"And is that…mistletoe?"

Rossa blinked. Sure enough, her mother was right – a sprig of mistletoe sat at the head of each fish, marking the corners of the square. And inside it were charcoal scratchings, almost like writing, as if done by a child, or…

A bear's claw.

Rossa turned her head this way and that, trying to make sense of the words, if indeed they were words. Then she rounded the table, and they became clear.

"My thanks," she read. "A blessed Yule to you and yours from Prince Boris, the Snow White Bear."

Her legs wouldn't hold her anymore, so Rossa sat down heavily on the nearest bench. His name was Boris, and he'd given her fish for Christmas. And, best of all…

"Thank all the angels and saints, he's not a knight," she breathed.

"No matter what that bear may be, it doesn't change what day it is. You're needed here, at the Christmas feast, not haring off after some bear in the woods," Mother said.

Rossa nodded. She wanted to run off after him, to ask a thousand, nay, a million questions, but her thoughts whirled too fast for even her to follow right now. It would be better to wait, until she'd had time to reflect. She'd make more sense then.

"And you need to be at your best. You are their lady, and they expect you to look your part. Go upstairs and bathe – your feast day gown is in my chamber, and you're not to come down until you're dressed and your hair is properly arranged," Mother said.

Yes. Rossa had seen the silk gown her mother had laid out, and she'd never dare venture into the woods wearing that. The dress was a death trap, with lace and ruffles and the neckline was so low every time she looked down, she could see her own breasts.

She didn't want to go into the forest wearing it. She didn't want to step into the great hall wearing it. Every man in the room would stare at her, thinking lustful thoughts, and, when they'd drunk enough of her mother's ale, some of them would talk about them, loud enough for her to hear. And her mother would not let her throw even a single fireball at them for it. Most unfair.

Men and their urges were the bane of her existence. No wonder she preferred the company of a bear.

"Yes, Mother," Rossa said.

But Mother wasn't finished yet. "When the winter is over and your father returns, I'll insist he take you to court. Whichever one suits you best, though I'll leave the choice up to him. When I was your age, I had a town to take care of, an estate to manage, and then a young son to raise. You have…nothing to hold you here. You should see some of the world, and find your place in it, for you're so much like your father. He was not content in the town where he grew up, either. There is a place in the world for you, Rossa. I don't know if it involves bears or princes or…things I've never seen, but can only dream of, but your father will be the one who can show you some of the world's wonders while you find it." She managed a smile. "Consider it my Yule gift to you. When your father comes home from the Emperor's court, he will take you, or we shall have words."

And while the world feared her father, Rossa knew her mother ruled his heart, so it would be as she decreed.

"Thank you, Mother," she said, her heart much lighter as she raced up the stairs. The gown was there, as impractical as she remembered, but she'd have to get used to such things if she was to go with her father to court. She'd have to learn to fight despite what she was forced to wear, or use weapons that did not depend on her agility or speed.

Like magic…

Thirty

When all the feasting and celebration was over, and Rossa was free to venture into the forest again, she still hadn't decided what to give Snow…or Boris…for his Yule gift. He'd given her fish, so food seemed fitting, but she brought provisions from the castle every day. What she should get him was fresh meat.

A deer, like the one she'd shot that first day she saw him, or a brace of those pilfering pigeons that had managed to elude her.

Though she'd love to bring him venison, once she'd remembered the pigeons, her ire rekindled at justice not yet served. Those pigeons needed to die.

Therefore, she resolved to go hunting first, so she might bring her kill to Boris in the afternoon. She checked the roost where she'd first found them, but the birds had not returned, likely frightened away by the beggar boy. So, she ventured deeper into the forest, sending her magic out before her, seeking them out.

After a couple of hours of searching and finding nothing, she began to suspect they'd been preyed upon by some of the mountain eagles and hawks that circled high above, looking for their next meal. Time to head back by a different route, and hope she encountered something that would make a better Yule gift than those pestilential pigeons.

But it seemed her new path was cursed, too, for she had not gone halfway before she began to hear loud cursing, which had clearly driven away the wildlife for miles around. What manner of idiot was out in the woods today? She definitely intended to give them a stern talking-to when she found them. Why, she wasn't even sure what some of those curse words meant…

The swearing seemed to come from the centre of a snow-covered bramble bush which alternated between shaking violently and staying unnaturally still. Someone had evidently become trapped inside the brambles and couldn't get out.

"Hello, do you need some help there?" Rossa asked.

"No!" came the angry response, followed by a few seconds where the bush moved as though caught in a high wind, before the swearing resumed, louder and more vociferous than before.

She longed to leave whoever it was to their fate, but her mother would have waded in with an axe to cut them free, before lecturing them on their use of foul language, and Rossa would do no less.

Sighing, she didn't need an axe, for she used magic to gently part the branches of the bramble bush until she'd formed a path to the centre of the patch so that the bush's captive might walk free.

Of course, it couldn't be that simple. The parted branches revealed a familiar snarling face over the same stained tunic – it was the beggar boy, whose matted hair was now hopelessly entangled in the brambles. Several bloody hanks of hair had already been claimed by the bush as trophies of their battle, and it didn't look like the beggar boy would win, even with her holding the branches back.

She'd have to go in after him.

Rossa drew her dagger and waded into the bush.

The boy didn't even seem to notice her until she started hacking at his hair, freeing him from the bush. He flailed at her, hitting her once more out of luck than any skill, and she saw red.

"Be still, idiot, or I'll leave you here for the carrion birds!" she hissed, then bit down on her lip and spelled him into stillness, rather than risk being hit again for helping this wretch.

Finally, she'd freed his hair from the brambles, though she'd shorn off a considerable amount in the process. She backed out of the bush, then a few yards more, before she released the spell paralysing him in place.

"You horrible, butchering witch! Look what you've done to my hair! Now I look like a fever victim, or a monk! How dare you lay hands on me, and cut my hair! Why, I should have you whipped for assaulting me so!" he howled.

Rossa folded her arms across her chest. "This horrible witch has just about had enough of you. I saved you from those brambles, and in about three heartbeats, I'm going to let go of the branches my magic is holding back, and you'll be trapped again, just like before, but I won't help you again, you ungrateful wretch!"

The boy's mouth dropped open in horror, silent for a long moment, before he spotted something on the ground that had his eyes widening with greed. Whatever it was, he snatched it up, then bolted out of the bushes and away, faster than Rossa cared to follow him.

Not a word of thanks, or an apology for his insults.

Next time, she told herself, she'd leave the boy in the bushes, and to blazes with him.

145

Thirty-One

The nightmare came again, as it always did. Every time, the dream was the same, and yet every time it was different, because in his heart he knew it was no dream – it was his reality, one he couldn't wake up from. Boris raced through the woods, his former squire chasing him with all the unnatural energy of a berserker in battle. Over and over, Igor would shout at him to just hand over the crown jewels, so that he could go home, but Boris knew there was more to it than that. If Igor got close enough to him, he'd attack, and there was no predicting those frenzied blows.

So far, Boris had been lucky, for his fur was thick and Igor's knife blade was short, so the boy hadn't wounded him anywhere that mattered yet. But he knew the boy wanted his head along with the jewels, for he'd said so often enough, and the stubborn squire would never stop. Couldn't stop.

And now there was Rossa, his Rose Red witch. If Igor found her, he'd try to use her against him. Use her as bait, to draw him out...

Because Boris would do anything to keep her from being hurt by the nightmares he'd run from, while vengeance for Vica and Lida's death slipped away from him, a little more each day, until he feared he didn't know the way back, would never find his treacherous brother, and his family's death would go unavenged.

He could not save Vica or Lida, but he could keep Igor away from Rossa, who deserved the protected castle life she was born to, with gorgeous gowns, glowing jewels, and blazing fires to keep her warm at night in soft beds befitting such a high lady.

Not life in a cave, or on the run, not knowing when Igor or Sviatopolk's soldiers might catch up to him, and kill him as well. Because he knew Igor could not survive out here on his own, so he must have help. At best, he was a clumsy scout, who reported back to better, more capable men, in such numbers that they could overwhelm a man on his own, like Boris was. He'd been hunting enough times to know claws were no match for well-forged steel held by well-trained hands.

So Boris didn't stop, didn't pause, didn't dare even return to the cave where he'd stashed the crown jewels, lest they catch him, or her…

The rush of a river ahead made him slow, then speed up again, bunching up his muscles so he might make the jump…

For a brief moment, Boris flew, before landing heavily on the snowy bank. He clawed his way up and over, running before he knew where he was, or where he was going.

Behind him, he heard Igor splash into the

river, swearing at the chill in the icy waters, but Boris didn't dare stop. Not yet. Maybe not ever…

Thirty-Two

It was with considerable pride and triumph that Rossa carried two brace of pigeons to Boris's cave. Yes, she was late bringing his Yule gift, but she'd been so preoccupied with hunting the pigeons to punish them for what they'd stolen, that she'd forgotten one of her father's most repeated tenets: that it was easier to make a mark come to you than chase it across the country.

So she found the sack of wheat they'd already ransacked, scattered it on the snow outside the barn, and waited. Within hours, she'd had a whole flock of pigeons to choose from, fattened on lowland wheat. She'd picked them off, one by one, until Sal promised her pigeon pie for supper, and she still had enough left over to take to Boris.

Yet the bear wasn't here, and hadn't been for some time. The ashes from his fire were cold, and there was no food left. The only thing remaining in his cave was a small pile of firewood and a lumpy sack she'd seen before, which she knew contained treasures like the brooch he'd given her on their first meeting, back in autumn. Old jewels she wished she could ask him about, for surely such treasures had a fascinating story behind them. As well as how they came to be here, in a cave in the mountains, guarded by a prince who'd been turned into a bear.

She waited and waited, but he didn't appear, and even when she sent her magic out questing for him, she found no bears at all. Perhaps he'd gone down to the river to catch some fish, for he was most skilled at that, if her Yule gift was anything to go by.

She'd never seen a bear fish. It would surely

be fun to watch.

So Rossa left the pigeons in the cave and set out for the river. She found the river easily enough, but still she didn't see a bear. Rossa had hunted all her life, but she'd never bothered to catch fish, so she hadn't the slightest idea where a good fishing spot might be. She followed the river upstream a way, until the banks grew too high and impassable, before heading down, toward the lake. The river grew deeper as streams joined it, widening as the banks became easier to traverse.

She fancied she heard a cry for help, then dismissed it.

Wait, there it was again.

She barrelled along the river bank, praying she'd be in time.

Then stopped and swore when she realised it was the beggar boy. This time, he was chest deep in the river, howling as something pulled him under, before he popped back up again, coughing and spluttering, before calling for help.

She knew she'd sworn not to help him, after

the last time, but she could hardly leave a boy to drown, no matter how ungrateful he was. Swearing, she stripped off her cloak and boots and waded into the water. It only came to her waist, but she was numb within moments – the boy was surely freezing. It was a wonder he was even alive.

It wasn't until she stood beside him that she saw the problem. A monster of a fish, easily twice as long as she was tall, had taken hold of his belt, and wasn't letting go. Every time it gave a mighty tug, the boy slipped under the surface, and had to fight his way up for another breath before the beast dragged him under again.

She tried to unfasten his belt, but it had swollen in the water, and her numb fingers could scarcely feel the belt, let alone work the knot free. Rossa pulled out her knife, and began sawing at the boy's belt. He was too busy fighting to breathe to notice, until she managed to cut through the belt and it floated free, dragged away in the maw of the monstrous fish.

Only then did the boy look down and let

out a wail: "You horrible witch! Now I have no belt to stop my tunic flapping in the wind…and you lost me my dinner! That fish would have fed me for a month!"

He spat in the water, then struggled to shore. When he climbed up the bank, he stopped long enough to make a rude gesture in her direction.

Rossa barely noticed, for the riverbed was slippery, and she struggled against the current on her numb feet. More than once, she slipped and landed face-first in the water, so she was soaking wet from head to toe by the time she reached the bank.

Only then did she realise that her cloak was gone – likely taken by the beggar boy turned thief, who was now nowhere to be seen.

Swearing and shivering, she did the only thing she could – head back to the bear's cave, to light a fire and hope it would be enough to warm her up and dry her wet clothes.

Thirty-Three

He heard her voice on the wind, and he thought he'd imagined it at first. But when he heard her call his name, he listened in earnest.

"So cold, Snow. So cold in the cave…"

He didn't think – he just reacted, breaking into a run, then a gallop, as four paws were faster than two.

He didn't stop until he reached the clearing.

Only then did he realise he'd been tricked, because it wasn't Rossa he saw, but Igor, holding the sack of treasures.

The last rays of the sun glinted on the

squire's dagger as he raised it, a mad grin on his face. "Now, all I need is your head and I'll be free!"

The boy berserker charged at him, slashing wildly.

For the first time in Boris's life, he let rage wash over him, until he felt almost as reckless as a berserker, too. How dare this boy try to trick him with Rossa's voice, that she was in danger. And stealing the crown jewels from him?

No. Boris was done running. This ended here and now.

He rose up to his full height. His first swipe sent the dagger spinning into the pond, to vanish beneath the icy waters. His second ripped out the boy's throat.

Gasping and choking, clutching at the bloody remains of his neck, the boy went down.

Boris dipped his paw in the pool to wash off the blood, before snatching up the sack of treasures to take it back to his cave.

Only then did he hear her voice again: "So cold, Snow…"

She was here.

Lying on her side in the cave, her clothes soaking wet, curled up and shivering in front of his empty fire pit.

She blinked and managed a weary smile. "Snow…"

He wished he could ask her what had happened. How she'd ended up all wet, without a cloak, out here in the forest.

Once again, she seemed to read his mind. "So…silly. A boy…pulled into the river…"

Igor had done this to her. Boris would have his head for this.

He pointed at the few sticks left in the woodpile, then outside, in an effort to tell her he was getting wood for the fire to help her get warm.

Rossa nodded.

Boris had never gathered wood so fast in his life. He pulverised two dead trees, then brought them, piece by piece, into the cave. He laid a fire in the fire pit, then looked for his flint. Had the boy stolen that, too?

Wishing he could curse aloud, Boris didn't know what to do. He had to get her warm, and without a fire…

Hesitantly, he lifted her in his arms, cradling her to his chest as he tried to wrap as much of his fur around her as possible.

"Why did you let the fire go out, Snow?" she asked sleepily.

She was too cold. If she slept…she might never wake.

Boris took her hand and stretched it toward the fire. He'd seen her throw balls of magic – could she do the same thing with fire?

"Silly bear," she said, then bit her lip. Fire spurted from her fingers, snaking around the branches in the firepit until they burst into flame.

Boris added more wood, willing it to burn.

"Cold. So cold and…draughty." She did something with her hands, and a small sphere appeared, growing larger. It passed through him with barely a tingle, and still it grew until it pushed against the cave walls. "Shield. Warm and…safe," she said. She nuzzled against his chest.

Boris didn't dare move. He just held her, and watched the flames, as her breathing grew even and the cold cave started to grow comfortably warm.

He'd give almost anything to be a man again. To hold Rossa in his arms, just the two of them…

When he was certain she was asleep, he leaned back, and tried to get some sleep of his own.

Because to sleep was to dream, and in his dreams he could kiss her as he held her, caress her with hands instead of claws, and she looked at him as a woman does a man, instead of a beast who deserved this fate, because he'd let his family die.

Thirty-Four

Somewhere in that foggy limbo between waking and sleep, she dreamed Snow returned, his warm arms encircling her as they had on Christmas Eve, his fur so soft she wanted nothing more than to stroke it, stroke him, all night.

She knew she'd slipped into a dream when he began to stroke her, too, and kiss her, but she didn't want to open her eyes, for that would end the dream. He peeled off her wet clothes, so that she was naked in his arms, but he didn't stop stroking, didn't stop kissing, leaving fire trails across her skin where he touched her, even with the warm, soft fur at her back telling her this was only a dream.

And then he placed the softest kiss on her thigh, higher than anyone else had ever touched, and her eyes flew open in surprise.

A white head sat between her thighs, her legs lifted over his shoulders, and then he kissed her again, higher still, before his fingers stroked her and she cried out, "Snow!"

He lifted his head and grinned at her, those same eyes in a human face, beneath hair so fair she'd thought it was white. "My sweet, sweet Rose. My true name is Boris, and you don't know how long I've dreamed of hearing your voice say it." His fingers stroked her again, slipping inside her.

A white bearskin cloak lay beneath her, as the man who'd worn it did the most delicious things with his hands and his tongue. She wanted this, more than anything she'd ever wanted in her life.

She wet her lips. "Boris." A spark of something shot deep inside her from where he touched her, setting her nerves afire, and she arched her back in pleasure. "Oh, Boris! My prince."

Dark soulful eyes regarded her, as his fingers never stopped moving, accompanied by the occasional kiss. Pleasure built and built, until it overflowed in an explosion of light.

"You don't know how long I've dreamed of you, like this," he said, his fingers already stroking her again.

Rossa did not want to admit it, but she'd dreamed of him, too, though she'd never been able to see his face. Now…

She tangled her hands in his hair – human hair, not fur – and dared to ask, "Was it this good in your dreams?"

He laughed softly, kissing her thigh again. "Nothing could compare to the wonder that is you, right here and now."

And as she screamed his name, she found herself without the breath to tell him she felt the same. But from the look in his eyes, she suspected he knew.

Thirty-Five

When the ache in his own loins proved almost too much to bear, Boris had to force himself to release her. If he pleasured her any more, he'd surely surrender to his own desires, and Rossa was a maiden still. Though whoever she married would be a very lucky man indeed.

He reached for her tunic. "This should be dry enough to wear now." He didn't dare meet her eyes as he handed it over. Couldn't even bring himself to watch her dress, though the image of her naked body, writhing with pleasure, would be one of his most treasured memories.

Rossa dressed silently, while he busied himself stoking the fire. He didn't want her getting cold again. He had to tell her, could not waste this opportunity when he had no idea how long he'd remain a man. The last time he'd been himself was the day Vica and Lida died.

"I was once a prince. My father's favourite son, though I had many brothers and sisters, and when he grew too old to defend our borders, he sent me out at the head of our army instead to fight back the raiders who invaded our villages. Then my father died, and my brother..."

He told her everything. How Vica and Lida had died, the potion he'd drunk, before taking the crown jewels. How he'd woken up in a cave, chased by the squire who'd betrayed him...

"I don't deserve any of what I lost, not any more. My family, the throne...even the crown now gathering dust in that bag of things. But I am a man, if only for a night, and I dream of what I do not deserve. A beautiful lady, who permitted me to save her, if only a little, and to love her, as much as I am able, but I am…nothing now. A usurper sits upon the throne that should have been mine, and instead of seeking vengeance for my family, for my father, I fled with the crown jewels, becoming the beast you called Snow. And though I might look like a man now, I am a beast still."

She frowned, then laid her hand on his arm and closed her eyes. Magic tingled at her touch, or maybe it was just because it was her, and then it was gone.

"The spell is still there. I feel it. I…" Her cheeks reddened, and she withdrew her hand.

Ah, she felt guilt for the intimacy they'd shared. Boris knew he should feel it, too, but if anything, he was already damned, so steeped in guilt he barely felt it any more.

"Forgive me. It was my passion, the heat of it that overwhelmed us both. The fault is mine," he said. If he could take her sins from her, he would. Heaven knew a few more wouldn't hurt him.

"No, it's…all through your tale, you kept

talking about your squire. The squire who is always watching you, hunting you. Did he see us…?" Her cheeks flamed as red as her name.

Boris shook his head. "No, he could not have seen us. Here, I'll show you." He held out his hand to help her to his feet, then wrapped his white bear skin cloak about her shoulders. He could not allow her to catch a chill. Only when she was properly dressed for the cold did he lead the way outside.

The moon sat high in the sky, casting its light down on the traitorous squire. The body lay beside the pool, but some night-time scavenger had dragged the boy's head several yards away, almost into the bushes.

"He will not bother you again," Boris tried to say, but no words came out. The only sound he could make was a growl.

He'd turned back into a bear.

Rossa stared in horror, her eyes darting from him to Igor and back to Igor again. "You did this? Slaughtered a starving boy I risked my life to save? He was a child – just a child! How could you, Boris? I trusted you – let you into my home, when all the while it was only a matter of time before you killed someone? You're wrong, you know. You're not a beast. A mindless beast, a creature of instinct, only kills for food, for survival. This…is the work of a monster, with the mind of a man. A monster who is not welcome in my mother's lands. If you are still here on the morrow, I give you fair warning, I will hunt you down and slaughter you like the monster you are. And then I will burn your body, for you do not even deserve a decent burial. Goodbye, Boris."

She turned on her heel and marched off into the dark night.

Boris raised a paw, wishing he could beg her to come back, but he no longer had the words. Even if he were a man again, he suspected there were no words he could say that would make her forgive him for what he had done. Even if he'd done it for her.

He wished he could weep, for what he had lost tonight. He'd touched heaven, only to be thrown into the pit for it. But even tears were denied him. It was what he deserved.

Thirty-Six

When Rossa woke the next morning, she was still simmering over the prince. He didn't even deserve a name, for he was no one to her. That she'd very nearly given him her maidenhead last night…was a kind of foolishness she didn't dare contemplate now in the light of the morning.

He was a monster who deserved to die. And, without her father here to dispatch him, she would do the deed. With relish.

Thick, woollen hose encased her legs, rough against her skin, in contrast to his soft caresses.

A thick linen tunic, topped by one of wool, before she buckled a leather breastplate over the breasts she'd let him kiss last night. Never again.

Her warmest cloak had vanished from the riverbank yesterday, likely stolen by the boy he'd slaughtered, but in its place hung a far superior one in unblemished, snowy white. She reached out to stroke the fur – as soft as she remembered it last night, for he'd laid her down upon it before making love to her. As a man, and not a bear, yet he'd been a bear again in the clearing with the body, so this fur had not been taken from him.

Maybe she should skin his corpse, and make a cloak from it, if only to remind herself of how close she'd come to disaster…

Or keep this one, so finely made, with fur on one side and thick lambswool on the other, for it would remind her of last night as well.

She would wear it while she hunted him, and while she killed him, so that she would remember his end as well as why he deserved it, she told herself, as she fastened the fur with the ruby brooch he'd given her on the day they first met.

The thick leather belt she slung around her hips would not cut as easily as the one she'd sliced off that poor beggar boy…was it only yesterday? Better for him to have drowned than the violent end he'd met at the end of Boris's claws.

Bloody bear. She'd seen him kill, but she'd wilfully forgotten how brutal he could be when he was with her. When he'd sat at her hearth, in her home. All so he could lull her into a false sense of security so…what? He could seduce her? She'd been so stupid…

But she'd found wisdom at last, even if it was too late for that boy. It was a lesson the bear would pay for with his lifeblood, she swore.

She pulled on her heavy boots, so that he would hear her coming and know he could not avoid her. That she would bring him down, place her boot on his neck, and list his crimes before delivering his death blow. Justice.

Her sword and her bow she left behind. If she found she needed them, magic would take the place of blade or arrow. She was a witch, born of a line of powerful magic users who were more than a match for any monster, magical or otherwise.

She dragged a comb through her hair, braiding it back tightly before coiling it on the back of her head. There would be no free curls for him to wrap around his finger as he kissed her, looking for all the world like he loved her, telling her she was the most beautiful woman he'd ever seen…

Enough! She screamed it silently at herself, for the traitorous thoughts invading her own head. Yes, the prince had made a tolerable lover for a night. That didn't change the fact that he was a murderer, and that he deserved to die.

She marched down the spiral stair, ignoring the grumble of her belly as the aroma of baking bread wafted up from the kitchens. She could break her fast when the deed was done, and not before. Lest she vomit up her breakfast on the snow, beside the bear's severed head.

Out the side door, through the gates, out to the…

Oh.

Outside the castle gate stood the monstrous white bear, carrying the corpse, the boy's head cradled in its lap.

He threw the body at her feet, then knelt down beside it to seize the head. He set it on top of the corpse's neck, as if the body were a puzzle that would come back to life, if he but pieced it together correctly.

"Have you come to turn yourself in? To confess your crime, so that my mother's guards will execute you, instead of me?" she demanded. Her heart ached as she hardened it against him, but she had no choice. She would not let him kill anyone else.

The bear shook its head violently, pointing at the corpse.

"Bringing him for a decent burial is the least you could do. They will not be lenient because of it. I shall see to that," she said. "You will still hang for – "

That's when she felt it. A whisper of magic, like the slightest breath of a breeze, between them. It wasn't the bear, and it wasn't her, which meant it had to come from the boy.

No. Corpses couldn't cast spells.

And yet…

She'd seen the ruin where the boy's throat had been last night. A dark hole, black in the moonlight, that appeared whole and healed now. If his head hadn't been severed, she might think…

The boy blinked. Then blinked again.

No. She'd imagined it. Surely.

"Where are the jewels? Give them back!" the boy demanded, staring at the bear. He tried to scramble to his feet, arms and legs flailing in the snow as the bear shoved him down with one massive paw, pinning him in place.

How…

Boris met her gaze and nodded, pleading for her to understand.

But what kind of monster didn't die when a bear decapitated it?

Absently, she sent a paralysis spell at the boy, like she had in the brambles, so he'd stay still without distracting her. If he was a boy, which she doubted.

Rossa closed her eyes, delving deep into the well of memories that weren't her own.

Generations of spellcasters, all adding to the great store of knowledge she could access if she looked hard enough. Someone must have seen such a monster, put a name to it…

Djinn. This…thing…was a djinn, a magic user who had betrayed their king, and been sentenced to serve as a slave until the debt of disobedience was paid. Trapped in the form in which they were enslaved, unable to die, until their king released them from bondage.

She stared into the boy's furious eyes. How had she missed the magic in his blood, for only a spellcaster could be punished so? Yet as she searched his body, she found no magic at all, in his blood or bones or anywhere except for the djinn curse that lay thick upon him like armour.

Boris had not cast this curse. No wonder he'd been running from this deathless thing, which could not be killed, relentless…

Nor had he slaughtered an innocent, defenceless child.

Her mouth suddenly dry, Rossa didn't know what to say. Boris deserved an apology, if her memories were correct, but she had to be sure...

"Take him to the barn. We'll question him there," she ordered.

Boris bowed, scooped up the boy, and followed her to the now pigeon-proof barn.

Thirty-Seven

Rossa issued orders like an army commander, and Boris could not do anything but obey. Within moments, she had Igor tied to a post in the barn, with a magical shield crackling around the walls so that no one would hear or see what went on inside. She cast a spell on Igor, too, telling him if he lied, his tongue would catch fire, so he had better tell her the truth.

Even Boris gaped a little at that. Surely the girl who condemned him for killing the boy would not torture him so.

Would she?

Then she enthroned herself on a sack of grain and began to question the squire.

Why was he hunting this bear?

What was the bear's real name?

Why did he betray the man he'd served?

Why did he poison him?

Igor's answers could have come from Boris's own lips, for the story matched his own. More than once, he found Rossa nodding, and relief began to trickle through his veins. If she believed him, maybe she'd forgive him. Maybe…

"I didn't poison him!" Igor shouted, straining at his bonds.

Rossa rose. "You gave him the drugged drink at the feast."

"Yes, but only because I was ordered to serve him that ale. I tried to warn him, tell him not to drink so much!"

She glanced at Boris, who nodded. The boy spoke the truth. If only he'd been more forthcoming at that long-ago feast, told him about the sleeping potion in his ale…

"Why didn't you tell him what was in it?"

she asked.

"I couldn't!"

"Why?"

But he clamped his mouth closed and shook his head. He would not – or could not – say.

"Did you know what the potion you gave him later would do?"

"No! Only that it was supposed to help him!"

Boris nodded again. So the boy had said, but he had not believed him then. Now…well, Igor's mouth was not ablaze, so he was telling the truth about his words then, but that didn't make those words true. He wished with all his might that he could be a man again, so that he could question the boy himself.

"Did you know the ale was drugged?" she asked.

The boy nodded.

"Why didn't you tell him? Your prince, the man you served, who you owed your loyalty to…why?"

"I couldn't!

"Why not?"

"Because the witch told me if I ever

breathed a word about the potion she put in the ale, it would be the last breath I ever took!" Igor exploded.

Then he began to wheeze, trying to suck in air that would not come. His face turned red, then blue, before he hung limp from the ropes that held him.

Rossa's mouth dropped open, and she darted forward to place her fingers on the boy's neck. "He's dead!"

Boris shook his head, but Rossa did not seem to notice, for she was too busy cursing.

She pointed at him. "You – stay here with him. I'm going to…I'll…I will return. Stay hidden. No one must know you are here." She marched out of the barn, sealing the door and the shield behind her, so he could not leave, even if he wanted to.

Sealed behind a shield, with Igor dead, and Rossa no longer out for his blood, Boris was safe for the moment. This time, he felt himself change.

He flexed his hands as Igor began to stir.

This time, Boris seated himself on Rossa's throne, where the boy's gaze landed the moment his eyes opened, before they widened with horror.

"How?" Igor managed to say.

Boris picked up a knife Rossa had left behind, and began to twirl it around his finger. "I'll ask the questions, boy. And if I don't like the answers…" He threw the knife into the air, and caught it, point down.

Igor swallowed. "What do you want to know?"

Thirty-Eight

By the time Rossa returned, Boris and Igor had reached an accord, though the boy was currently hanging limp for the third time, looking for all the world like the corpse he'd been out in the clearing. Except with his head still attached, of course. Rossa would not like it if he turned her barn into a slaughterhouse.

"I brought some breakfast. I thought you might be hungry," she said, her eyes on the tray in her hands. When she glanced up, she nearly dropped it. "You're…not a bear!"

Boris grinned. "No. I'm not sure how it

happened. Perhaps it's something about being inside your shield, but I feel...more like myself."

Rossa hurriedly set the tray down and laid her hand on his arm again. She shook her head. "Yet I can still feel the spell inside you. The bear isn't gone, only...sleeping, or something. As if waiting for the opportunity to emerge..."

Boris might not be a witch, but he'd come to a similar conclusion. "Oh, there's a purpose for it, all right. I will need its strength to drag that usurper off my father's throne and make him pay for the lives he's taken. After he's freed Igor from his curse, of course, which is why he's going to help me."

Rossa shot a sceptical glance at the lifeless boy. "You'll need to resurrect him, and get a few decent meals into him first. He's hardly in any shape to attack a king at the very heart of his power. Why, there'd be guards, knights, courtiers...he'd have no chance. Not even with your help. One bear against a company of guardsmen...I've never been to court, but even I know that is suicide."

"Come with me." Even as the words left his lips, he wished they hadn't. He'd lost the woman he loved once to Sviatopolk. He wouldn't put Rossa in danger as well.

A wry smile curved her lips. "A bear, a beggar boy and a maiden with a bow. Oh, the bards will make ballads about us, filling every court in the land with gales of laughter that anyone could do something so stupid." She took a deep breath. "And yet…you will need me, I think. But even then, we might not be enough. If you want the king to listen, without killing us on sight, you'll need someone else. What we need is my father. He'll know what to do."

Boris opened his mouth to ask what some country baron could do against a king, but Igor took that moment to suck in an enormous, gasping breath, drawing Rossa's eyes to him.

"Is it true? Will you swear to serve Prince Boris again, as you did before, and help him right the wrongs that were done to him? Even if it means killing the king?" Rossa demanded.

Igor wet his lips. "I will."

"Will you swear not to harm Prince Boris,

or anyone else unless I order you to do so? Will you promise not to run away if I untie you?"

"To all of it, I swear, my lady," Igor said.

She snapped her fingers, and the ropes around the boy slithered away to coil themselves up like a nest of snakes in the corner.

"And if I ordered you to go get a meal and a bath and clean clothes, as befitting your station as Prince Boris's squire, would you obey?"

"Gladly, my lady." Igor bowed low.

Boris hadn't noticed, but the sulkiness that had annoyed him so much before was gone from Igor's voice and expression now. How long had it been? Had he been running for years?

Boris glanced down at his clothes. He hadn't seen this tunic since the day Lida and Vica died, and it still bore traces of their blood. "Lady Rossa, might I trouble you for a bath and a change of clothing, too?"

She eyed him thoughtfully. "I'll see what I can find. We don't see many princes here in the mountains, so it may not be as fine as you are used to. At least until the passes open in spring, and my father will return."

That was at least a month away, maybe two! Boris swallowed. As a bear, he might attempt to traverse snowy mountain passes, but as a man, he'd likely die in the attempt. Even Bisseni berserkers weren't crazy enough to cross the mountains in winter.

After so long as a bear, he felt somehow diminished to stand before her as a man. Yet he bowed as low as he had dozens of times before. "I will be most grateful for whatever hospitality you offer, my lady."

When he straightened, he found Rossa blinking at him in bemusement. "Yes, I'll have to find you a bed, too, I suppose." And with that, she led the way out of the barn, gesturing for them both to follow.

Thirty-Nine

When Rossa rounded the corner and reached the kitchen gardens, she knew something was wrong. Too many people bustled about, fetching and carrying with a feverish intensity that told Rossa they feared the consequences if they failed in their task.

"What is it? What has happened?" she demanded of the nearest man.

"The master has arrived! Everything must be made ready!" He excused himself and hurried off.

The master? The only master Rossa knew

was her father, in his role as Master Assassin. But he couldn't possibly be here – the passes were still blocked by snow, and would be for months yet.

Mother would know. Whoever was here, they would not have arrived without her knowledge. And at this hour, as she was usually to be found in the solar they used for a dining chamber instead of the draughty great hall, that's where Rossa headed.

Sure enough, Mother wasn't alone – a man and a woman stood before her, cloaked against the cold, for the fire had only recently been lit.

The man's grey cloak seemed to blend in with the wall behind him, so that her eye was drawn away from him, dismissing him, but the woman's cloak of regal purple was as vibrant as flowers in the spring. A member of the Emperor's family, perhaps? For surely only royalty could afford such costly dye.

"Rossa, I was just about to send someone to summon you," Mother said.

The pair turned, and the grey man pushed his hood off his head.

"Father!" she exclaimed, rushing to hug him.

It wasn't until she pulled away from him that she felt the purple woman's eyes on her.

Amethyst eyes, like nothing Rossa had ever seen before. Drawing her in, as if with a powerful enchantment she could not resist…

Father coughed, and the spell was broken, if indeed it was a spell. "Rossa, you won't believe where I found your fairy godmother. We got to talking about you, and the more we talked, the more we agreed that it was time she paid you a visit, so she cast a portal, and here we are." He spread his hands wide. "Lady Zuleika, your god-daughter, Rossa. And Rossa, this is Zuleika. My niece."

Lady Zuleika managed a nervous smile and ducked her head. "I'm still new to this. My mother Zoraida – Master Zoticus's sister – died only recently, and I am still learning the full extent of her duties as fairy godmother. I'm sorry I haven't come to help you yet, but you seemed to be doing all right, not in need of my help yet, until Uncle told me of his vision…"

Father waved her into silence, which only intrigued Rossa more. She knew Father had visions of the future, but she'd never heard him having one about her.

"Ah, I'm not the only one who brought an important guest. Prince Boris, have you come to see the holy relics?" Father asked, striding past Rossa.

How could she have forgotten Boris and Igor?

Boris's eyes darted about, as if seeking an escape — not an uncommon response for someone meeting her father for the first time, as his reputation often preceded him — before he decided to hold his ground and offer a nervous smile to Father. "Forgive me, sir, but I do not recall where we met before today."

Father's smile was genuine, as he shook his head. "No, forgive me, Your Highness. It's just that you are so like your likeness in the cathedral, I recognised you instantly. A man with your reputation would surely have come here to pray over the holy relics my wife's ancestors brought back from their most holy crusade. The relics of the Holy Innocents, no less! It is no wonder you sought them out."

"I..." Boris seemed as lost for words as

Rossa herself.

"You must stay here in the castle, with us, if Lady Sara does not object. Only our best guest chamber is good enough for such a prince!" Father said.

Mother moved to stand at Father's side, repeating his offer. Before Rossa could object, Mother whisked Zuleika, Boris and Igor off to show them their chambers.

Leaving her alone with Father. Whose gaze remained fixed on her, as he smiled, waiting for her to ask the questions that burned her tongue.

"Do you...Father, how do you know Boris?" she asked.

His smile widened. "Oh, his reputation is well-known. As a warrior, as a leader, and there are those who say he is a saint. Quite a remarkable man. I have always wondered...and now I have seen him with my own eyes. A remarkable man indeed."

A man she'd called a monster. Which she still hadn't apologised for...

Rossa ducked her head, not wanting to meet her father's eyes. Gah, she'd been so stupid. It was a good thing Father had left her at home.

"With your godmother's help, we will leave for court on the morrow. With Prince Boris, for I have an inkling he might want to leave earlier than the spring," Father said. He patted her shoulder. "If you have any suitable court clothes, you'll want to bring them, so you'd best go upstairs and pack."

"Yes, Father." Rossa was halfway up the stairs to her tower before she thought to question how Father knew all the things he did. Yet she didn't dare return downstairs to ask, lest he reconsider letting her go with him.

Finally, Father believed she was ready, though Rossa herself felt far from it.

Forty

What Father had meant, Rossa discovered the next morning, was that she would need to dress for court before leaving the castle, for Zuleika could cast magic portals that allowed her, and those accompanying her, to travel instantly from one place to another. Having nothing better than the red gown she'd worn at Christmas, Rossa had put that on, which Father had insisted on ornamenting with a ruby necklace that weighed more than the belt she'd sheathed her daggers in only yesterday. Father had brought her a new cloak from

Byzas, in a deep wine red that rivalled Zuleika's for its brightness. She'd fastened it with the brooch Boris had given her, though she dreaded what her father might say when he saw it.

Boris and Igor wore clothes Mother must have found for them, all of which were very fine, yet Boris had chosen to wear his white bear skin cloak, and a crown she knew had come from the sack of treasures he'd kept in the cave. She hadn't looked too closely at it before, but now it sat in his pale hair, woven strands wrapping around his head, with a single sparkling stone in the middle of his forehead. A diamond, surely, though it was as clear as water and drank the light, sending out rainbows when the sun hit it. He looked every inch a prince.

Father chose grey, as always, but she recognised his grey finery as distinct from the grey travelling clothes he'd worn yesterday. The only jewels he wore were on his weapons, and even they were few. The king might have made him a lord in name when he married her mother, but Father himself had not changed a bit because of it.

Zuleika had refused to wear any but her own clothes, and, to Rossa's surprise, Father had simply nodded and left it at that. Zuleika was younger than Rossa, Rossa had discovered, but the ease with which she created the portal to take them to the court in Buda demonstrated that she was a far more powerful enchantress than Rossa would ever be.

Zuleika's portal had barely faded before she said, "This is where I leave you, for I am needed at another court today. It is a small matter, regarding a ball and some shoes that shall be lost, but it is nevertheless of the utmost importance. Should you have need of me, I believe my other god-daughter will no longer need my services after midnight, so I shall return then." Before any of them could say a word, she cast another portal and was gone.

Rossa looked askance at Father, who merely shrugged and said, "My mother and my sister were forever flitting about the world, seeing to the affairs of their various godchildren. My sister fought a dragon for her godson once. To hear her tell the tale, it was more of a skirmish than a battle, which did not last long, but I have it on good authority that everyone else who fought the dragon died, right up until the day someone finally slayed the dragon. As she says, if we need her, she'll be here after midnight. I'm sure we'll survive a day without her." Father offered his arm, and Rossa took it. "Let's go see the king."

<h1 style="text-align:center">Forty-One</h1>

"This is not Prislav," Boris said, surveying the city walls. "I have never seen this city before."

Master Zoticus, as Rossa's father had insisted he was called, shrugged. "You have been away some time, Your Highness. The new king felt a new capital would be best, and he now rules from here in Buda. While we are here, you must allow me to show you your likeness in the cathedral. Beautiful work, though you will have to tell me if it does your brother David justice."

Boris closed his eyes. David. How long had

it been since he'd thought of him? David deserved justice as much as Vica and Lida, and still Boris had not delivered it. His family deserved better. He clenched his fingers around the hilt of the sword he'd borrowed from the castle armoury. Lady Sara had said the blade had belonged to one of her ancestors who'd gone on a holy crusade to free the Holy Land, and that the man's spirit would surely be happy to see it in his hand.

In truth, it felt foreign to hold a blade again, when his claws had been his weapon of choice for so long. The bear roared within him, like a creature with its own mind, eager to be unleashed on Sviatopolk.

Rossa and her father led the way to the throne room, but when they reached the doors, Zoticus stopped to speak to the herald, while Boris did not stop. He would no longer endure a usurper on his father's throne.

"Prince Boris of Rostov, with Lord Zoticus and his daughter, Lady Rossa," the herald announced.

The people parted, bowing as they cleared the way for Boris. He saw fear in their eyes, and so they should fear him. They'd supported a false king, a murderer, who did not deserve the throne.

He did not stop until he reached the foot of the dais where the king sat. Guards stood on either side of him, hands on their spears in readiness to defend the king, but Boris would not let them stop him. He'd broken larger branches than those spears with a single swipe of his paw.

He planted his feet, widening his stance, knowing the moment he beheld his brother's face, rage would take over and he would become a bear again, but this time, he was ready for it. He prayed that Zoticus would shield Rossa's eyes from the carnage.

Only then did he raise his eyes to meet the king's.

"You're not Sviatopolk!" Boris blurted out.

Forty-Two

"You're not Sviatopolk!"

For a moment, the king looked surprised, before he burst out laughing. The rest of the court followed his example. Father remained silent, and Rossa did the same. This was politics, which her father knew far better than she ever would.

"I thank heaven I am not Sviatopolk the Cursed every day, and I'm sure my subjects do, too!" the king said.

Boris just stood there, shocked, and Rossa's heart went out to him. Her father had evidently brought them to the wrong court. He should step forward and say something, instead of leaving Boris to bear the ridicule for his mistake.

It was almost as though Father had read her thoughts, for he strolled forward, keeping her hand firmly on his arm until a few steps before the dais. Only then did he let go, offering the king a courtly bow before he said, "Your Majesty, Prince Boris here has spent many years in search of the missing crown jewels, stolen by Sviatopolk the Cursed. I believe he has finally found news of them, which we would like to share with you, in private."

The king regarded Father for a long moment. Finally, he said, "If you have indeed found the lost crown jewels, then I would be greatly in your debt, Lord Zoticus."

Father winced. No, he did not like that title. The king only grinned, as if he knew this all too well.

"This audience is over. We shall resume on the morrow. See that refreshments are brought for our guests," the king said.

He led the way behind the throne, to a

smaller, more intimate audience chamber. One where there were chairs clustered around a table, none more ornate than the others, though the king took the one at the head of the table.

"Lady Rossa, you must come and sit beside me. If I had known Lord Zoticus had such a beautiful daughter, I would have summoned him to court sooner." Desire burned in the king's eyes.

This old man was as bad as the boys of Mirroten. Rossa regretted that he wasn't the traitor Boris wanted to kill, for her fingers itched to send a fireball at him. Or maybe a gust of wind so icy, it froze off certain parts he surely no longer needed…

"She's an enchantress, Bela, and you'd be playing with fire you cannot begin to imagine," Father drawled as he took the seat at the king's left hand.

Rossa felt her cheeks grow hot. Even with her father there, the king was still staring at her.

"But she's your daughter. Any heirs she gave me would be the most well-guarded children in the world. No one would dare harm them..." the king breathed. "Give me an heir, Lady Rossa, and I will give you a crown, and name you Queen Regent upon my death."

Give him an heir? Have sex with this old man? Rossa wished she hadn't eaten breakfast, because she was about to vomit it up all over the king's costly carpet. Boris was the only man she'd ever considered allowing into her bed, and to share herself with anyone else...

"He may not be Sviatopolk, but say the word, Lady Rossa, and I will defend your honour with my blade. If you desire a crown, you have only to ask and I will give it to you," Boris said. He glared at the king. "Freely, for I ask nothing in return." He took the seat at the foot of the table, opposite the king.

Rossa swallowed, then slid into the seat between her father and Boris.

"I believe you would benefit more by talking about crowns with Boris, instead of my daughter, Bela. That's why I brought him," Father said, his tone edged with irritation.

"Fine," the king sighed. "Tell me, Boris, what do you know of Sviatopolk the Cursed, and the treasures he stole?"

"Sviatopolk was my bastard brother. He stole my wife and daughter from me, ordering them to be murdered, and I suspect he killed my father and my brother, David, too. He did not deserve the crown he stole from my father. So after he took everything from me...I took everything from him," Boris said. He lifted his sack of treasures onto the table, but he did not spill the contents. Instead, he seemed to be fixated on the king. "You're wearing my brother's crown."

King Bela touched the plain gold coronet on his head. "This was forged for King Yaroslav the Wise, after he and his army drove Sviatopolk out of the capital. It has been passed down through my family for generations."

Boris shook his head. "No. My brother Yarik was given that crown on the day our father sent him to govern the north, while I was sent south to deal with the Bisseni raiders. He was Prince Yaroslav, then, my half brother. I suppose with my brother dead, me gone, and Sviatopolk a murderer and a traitor, the next in line for the throne would be Yarik, but…where is he now? He would have sent men out to find me, he said he supported me as the next king…" Boris trailed off. "How long have I been gone?"

Father winced. "Maybe we should have gone to the cathedral first. The likeness is quite remarkable. I imagine the artist must have known Prince Boris very well."

The king's jaw dropped. "Do you mean to say…this is Saint Boris? And he somehow miraculously preserved the crown jewels, so that he might return what his brother stole?" He stared at Boris in wonder.

The men kept talking, but Rossa's mind would not stop whirling. She'd known Boris's story sounded familiar, but she'd never considered it might be the tale of a two hundred years dead saint. And yet…

The clang of metal on the table dragged Rossa out of her reverie. Crowns, jewels…the sack of treasure just sat there in an undignified jumble. Tarnished from age, kept in a sack for two centuries…

"My grandfather said the treasures had likely

been melted down and sold, to pay for the civil war that erupted when Yaroslav died. For he might have been a wise king, but his sons fought like rabid dogs, killing each other off until none remained. My grandfather was descended from one of Yaroslav's daughters, who married a foreign prince. She attended her father as his nurse in his final days, and she wrote an interesting account of that time. His mind was so far gone that he imagined he and not Sviatopolk the Cursed had commanded that his father and brothers and their heirs be killed, and he had only framed Sviatopolk in order to claim the throne for himself. Perhaps it is true. I do know it was he who petitioned for Boris and David to be proclaimed saints, their bodies buried in the cathedral he built in their honour. I have seen the tombs myself."

"Has anyone ever opened them?" Father asked. "Because I would wager Boris's tomb is empty, or contains someone other than the saint."

The king scratched his chin. "What would you be willing to wager?"

"How long?" Boris demanded.

Both men stared at him.

"How long ago did your two saints die?"

Neither man seemed inclined to answer, so it fell to Rossa. "Two hundred years," she whispered.

"No! I swore I would bring them justice. That I would execute the man who ordered them killed. He can't be dead. He can't!" Boris rose so quickly, he knocked his chair over, but he did not stop to right it before he stormed out of the room.

Rossa rose to follow him.

Father put a restraining hand on her arm. "Let him go. It's a lot for any man to take in."

Rossa shook him off. "You knew, or at least you suspected. You should have told him, instead of letting him find out like this. And you." She pointed a damning finger at the king. "You laughed at him, before the whole court. A court that should be his, not yours, stolen by your ancestor's treachery. That man is our rightful king, and I will not just let him go!" She marched out the door, across the throne room, and out into the main square.

She had to find him. She had to.

Forty-Three

The cathedral was so grand, it rivalled the palace. Inside, it was even more ornate. Mosaics covered the walls, floors and even the ceiling, showing scenes he remembered hearing about in the much smaller church in Prislav, when he'd been a boy.

The altar at the far end stood amid the most brightly coloured pictures, but in the wings on either side of it were the Virgin's altar…and the one that was usually dedicated to the church's patron saint. The saint's altar was what drew Boris, for what he both hoped and dreaded he would find there.

Two stone coffins flanked him, each bearing a carved likeness of a man on top. Boris could not bear to look. He found himself on his knees, the mosaic floor rising up to meet him until his forehead kissed the cold tiles.

And he wept.

For two hundred years wasted. That Vica had not had a better husband, or Lida a better father. That Sviatopolk had won, and it had fallen to Yarik to avenge them. That they'd made him a saint, when he wasn't fit to scrub the floors in this church, let alone enter heaven.

Light footsteps padded on the tiles behind him. He wanted to snarl at the priest or whoever it was to leave him. Boris felt the bear rise within him, ready to vent his fury on anyone who helped to maintain this mockery.

"Do you want me to open the coffins?" Rossa asked, her voice quiet and calm to the storm raging inside him.

No, he did not want to see David's face in death. He, at least, deserved sainthood, so his remains would be incorruptible. But to look upon his face, to have to admit his failure…no, Boris did not have the strength for it.

But he also didn't dare admit that to Rossa. She'd come here to help him fight for justice for David, and he could not bear for her to think him a coward. And yet…that's what he was. He'd been running for nigh on two hundred years, instead of delivering the justice he'd promised.

"Well, I'm not waiting any longer. I want to see what's inside. So if you won't do it, I will."

The scream of stone scraping against stone set his teeth on edge, until a final clunk told him she'd set the coffin lid down.

"Looks like the artist carved him from life. The statue on top is holding a book, and so is he. Huh. I'd heard saints' bodies don't decay, but it's strange to see it. I would have thought he'd be a skeleton by now, but…Boris, is this your brother?"

Boris swallowed. Of course Rossa had the courage to look upon David's dead body. And if a maiden could do it, what did that make him?

He rose. Never had three steps seemed so

far before, but he forced himself to take each one, until he could clutch the lip of David's tomb. He took a deep breath, and looked down.

The boy he'd remembered had become a man, and a monk, too, judging by the robes he'd been buried in. His hands were clasped together as if in prayer, over a book of psalms that had once belonged to their mother.

Boris's mouth went dry. He would have given anything to prevent David's death, but looking at his brother now, so peaceful, Boris didn't begrudge him his place in heaven. Though Boris had broken his oath to avenge his brother, he had the feeling the man who had briefly lived in this body would forgive him for it.

"I'm sorry, David," he whispered.

"What for? You didn't kill him. Didn't even know he was in danger, or surely you would have warned him. Or dealt with the danger. Why should you be sorry?"

Her words felt right, somehow, and yet he could not accept them. "I'm sorry I didn't deliver justice to his killer."

Rossa blew out a breath. "If it's any consolation, it seems the killer met a sticky end, anyway. Sviatopolk the Cursed did not keep his crown for long, and he did not live long after he lost it. If I remember my history rightly, a company of the Varangian Guard caught up with him and slaughtered him slowly, over several days. Father said he's been asked to do something similar on occasion, when his target deserves a slow death. He said he usually suggests they hire an executioner instead."

Boris closed his eyes. Sir Cyril would have taken command, and hunted him down. For him. Because they believed he was dead…

He scrubbed at his eyes. Cyril and his men were long dead, much like everyone he'd ever known. But to do such a thing for him…he could never repay them. Where he had failed, Cyril had succeeded. Of course he had.

"So, ready to open the other box, to see what's inside?" Rossa asked. She bit her lip, then stared at David's final resting place. The lid slid back into place, sealing his remains inside.

Would Boris ever be ready? He feared the answer was no, but he could not say it. Thank the heavens Rossa had the strength to open them when he could not.

He bowed to David's memory, before turning to face his own grave. At least when a man looked upon his own mortality, he was supposed to feel some apprehension. Even Rossa wouldn't judge him for suppressing a shiver.

"Right, here goes," she said. This time, she lifted the lid clean off, and set it against the wall. "Oh, that's…most unnerving. No wonder the mosaic likeness is so much like you."

Boris dared to open his eyes. Unnerving was an understatement – he found himself staring at his own sleeping form, or so it seemed. "How is this possible?" he breathed.

Rossa frowned. "There's magic here. A spell, so light I can barely sense it. It feels like…a glamour, for that uses hardly any power at all. I should be able to remove it, if you just give me a moment…there!"

The Boris in the box vanished, to be replaced by a vision he'd never thought to see again. Vica lay there in his stead, holding Lida to her breast, as if they'd both fallen asleep only a moment ago. Not as though, two hundred years into the past, they'd been sent screaming into a death they hadn't deserved. While he did nothing, like the illusion someone had laid over them.

"Was she…your wife?" Rossa asked, her tone almost timid.

Boris nodded. "Princess Slavica, though I called her Vica, and our daughter, Lida. They look like they might wake at any moment." But they wouldn't, he knew. And he did not want them to, for if they did wake, they would condemn him for letting them die, and rightly so.

"They're both so beautiful, though little Lida looks more like you, I think. You must miss them very much. I'm so sorry." Rossa wiped away a tear, then laid her hand on top of his.

It was on the tip of his tongue to ask her what she was sorry for, as she certainly hadn't killed them. Hadn't even been born while they lived and breathed. And while his heart still ached with loss as he looked at his family, it wasn't the same stabbing sensation it had once been. He'd said his farewells, and he knew Vica would never look at him with love again. That if he reached down to touch them, they would be as cold as the stone bed their bodies now occupied. Instead, he was becoming increasingly distracted by the warm hand on his. The living, breathing woman at his side, who knew his past, and all his failings, and still she stood beside him.

She wasn't looking down into the past, at the family he'd lost. No, she gazed upward, at the ceiling. "Whoever made this did a masterful job. Your brother's staring up at heaven, but you're watching over your family. As if the artist knew who truly lay in this coffin, though he's made your face exactly as it looked in the illusion…"

For the first time, Boris dared to look up, and what he saw had fury erupting in his chest. "I'm not some benevolent saint, watching over anyone. Whoever made that didn't know me at all. When it came down to it, when they really needed me, I could not protect them. Could not…" He buried his face in his hands and wept.

There. Now she would see him as he truly was, and leave him to his misery. He should have used that dagger the day they died, instead of dishonouring them by running…

Rossa's arms came around him, pulling him into an embrace. For a girl half his size, she had surprising strength. "You saved me. Twice. I'm not sure I ever thanked you properly for that. I'm certain you would have saved them if you could, and that artist knew it, just as they knew you were not buried in that box with them. There are witches who see the future. My grandmother did. Perhaps the artist saw something that has not happened yet, and that's what's on the wall. Not what was, or what is…but what will be."

Boris shook his head. "No, it can't be. I failed her. Failed them. What woman could ever love me, knowing I could not protect her? Or our children?"

He felt her stiffen in his arms.

"Well, I…I…I think if you kept your promise to Igor, and helped to break the curse your brother had cast on him, you'd at least demonstrate that you can save a child. That…that would be something." She pulled away from him, then waved her hand to close the coffin.

The quiet clunk of the stone falling into place over them sounded so final, Boris wanted to reach out and shove it open again. To see their faces again, just one last time…

"We should return to the castle," Rossa said, her tone cold.

Loss slid through his insides, leaving him empty. He'd lost Vica and Lida, but why did it feel like he'd lost Rossa, too?

Forty-Four

When Rossa and Boris returned to the audience chamber, it was like they'd never left. Father and the king had a jug of wine between them, as they laughed over something one of them had said.

"Where's Igor?" Rossa asked.

Both men shrugged, and the king sent a servant in search of the boy. When he arrived, flanked by two guards, they said they'd found him in the castle kitchens. He'd remained in the throne room after everyone else had left, and when the guards had tried to throw him out, he'd told them he was the squire to the prince currently meeting with the king, so they couldn't, and one of the serving maids took him to the kitchens, where he'd eaten enough for three men and was well on his way to finishing a fourth portion when they found him.

When Igor saw the king, he fell to his knees. "Please, Your Majesty. I brough him back, and the crown jewels, just like you told me to. Please lift the curse."

King Bela frowned at the boy. "That is not an order I recall giving."

"But it was you. You're all old now, and fat, but you're wearing the same crown and you're still the king," Igor persisted.

That's when Rossa knew that an old man's deathbed ramblings had not been ramblings at all, but a confession. Which meant all these years, Boris had blamed the wrong brother, and the one who'd been called wise had deserved to die more horribly than the one they'd called cursed.

"I can do it," Rossa blurted out. "I just need a drop of your blood, Your Majesty. To break the spell."

It would take his blood and some of hers, and possibly the crown, for djinn were enslaved to an object, and for Igor to recognise a crown after so many years…it fit, in a dark, twisted way. The crown that had belonged to the brother Boris had trusted, who had betrayed him and the rest of their family…

"And I need to touch your crown, if only for a moment."

The king's eyebrows rose. "Do you hear that, Zoticus? Your daughter asked me to give her a crown. I believe I win that wager." He took off the coronet and held it out to her.

She refused to take it. "Blood and your crown, King Bela. Your ancestor enslaved this boy for two centuries, after he stole the throne he passed down to you. This is not about you or me, but about righting wrongs that never should have happened."

Father drew his dagger, and held the blade out to the king. King Bela pricked his finger on the point, then let a dark drop fall onto the hammered gold. Then a second, and a third, before he stuck his finger in his mouth and sucked it. "Now will you show me some magic?" he mumbled around his finger.

Rossa fought down her laughter. "Yes."

Father held out his dagger to her, and she ran the back of her hand across the blade, until a line of blood beaded her skin. She swiped the bleeding cut across Bela's crown, blending the king's blood with her own. Now she held the crown, she could feel the magic threads that tied it to Igor. One by one, she severed them, until the boy was free.

Igor drew in one great, gasping breath. "I can't believe it! Is it really gone?"

"Igor, take out your dagger, and stab yourself in the arse," Rossa said.

"No!" Igor snapped.

Rossa tossed the crown back to the king. "It is done. If the spell had not been broken, he would not have been able to refuse. Now, I believe the throne owes this boy a debt. Especially as he is partially responsible for restoring the crown jewels to you."

King Bela's frown deepened. "What would you ask of me, boy? What is it that you want?"

Igor stared at each of them for a long

moment, before he turned to face the king. "All I ever wanted was to be a knight. I'd only just begun to be Prince Boris's squire. I thought I would only spend a few years as a squire, with some training, and then I'd be allowed to become a knight."

"Perhaps Prince Boris…" the king began.

"NO!" said Igor, Boris and Rossa, all at the same time.

"Your Majesty, Igor has spent two hundred years hunting Prince Boris so he could bring his head back to…your ancestor, and Boris has spent the same amount of time fighting him off. As Prince Boris is still firmly attached to his head, he might not be the best teacher for the boy. Perhaps another knight…" Rossa suggested.

King Bela nodded. "I believe I can find a suitable knight to train you." He turned to the guards, who hadn't yet left. "Take him to the barracks hall, where the other squires are quartered, and see that he has a bed."

Out they went, leaving only four of them in the room.

The king leaned forward, his eyes on Rossa.

"What would I have to offer you, for you to give me an heir, Lady Rossa? Name it, and it shall be yours. Your father refuses to bargain on your behalf, even wagering that you will not agree. That a crown is not enough. So, assuming I will already give you a crown, what else could you possibly want?"

Rossa glanced at her father. He met her gaze, looked at Boris, then winked at her.

She hoped he hadn't wagered anything he didn't want to lose.

"A boon," she said finally. "If you would grant me the right to ask for anything at all, at any point in the future, and you must give it to me…then I shall give you your heir."

A smile flashed across Father's face for a moment, before it disappeared, as though it had never been. Certainly too fast for the king to see it, for he was fixated on her.

"You shall have it, Lady Rossa. And I shall commission a crown made just for you. Any jewel you wish, wrought in whatever shape you desire. Tonight, we shall have a feast to celebrate – "

"The announcement of your heir, Prince

Boris," Rossa interrupted. "Say he is your son, or your nephew, for no one will believe that he is your many-times-great-uncle. You shall say he has only just returned from his successful quest to return the crown jewels that were stolen so long ago. A man proven in battle, trained to rule…of your own blood, as royal as you yourself…who was denied the throne because of your ancestor's treachery. For him to return when you are without an heir is fortuitous for you both – perhaps some might say it is fate, or even divine intervention. Invoke Saint Boris, if you wish. I give you the only rightful heir to your throne."

Father began to clap. "Well played, daughter. What say you, Bela?"

The king did not look pleased. "I had hoped…" He sighed. "Very well. I defer to the wisdom of Lady Rossa. Who would make a brilliant queen, though it is not to be." He rose. "What say you, Prince Boris? Though you are a saint, and my many-times-great uncle, though my ancestor betrayed you…would you agree to assume the throne, upon my death?"

Boris stared at the king for what seemed like

forever. Finally, he said, "I came here, with my friends, to kill the man who sat on my father's throne. Now you're offering it to me upon your death. Perhaps this is why my father died, far sooner than any of us wished. Do you desire death, King Bela?"

Bela gave a wry smile. "No, I do not. I'd like to think I have at least a few years left to live. Maybe many more."

Boris dropped to one knee. "Then we are in agreement. I will agree to be your heir, as long as you mean to live many years yet."

Bela's gaze grew wistful. "I wish I had been blessed with a son like you. I'm sure your father would have been proud of the man you have become."

Boris inclined his head. "In everything, I strove to make my father proud, and I honour his memory now when I ask you, in proclaiming me as you heir, you also declare me to be your only son. A clear succession is the easiest way to avoid civil war. The kingdom I remember was a strong one, and I mean to help you keep it so."

"Then we should send word to the kitchens,

that tonight there shall be a grand celebration feast for the whole court, and in the meantime, allow me to bring you up to date on the history you might have missed…"

Bela led Boris off to his private chambers, leaving only Rossa and her father in the room.

Rossa swallowed. Her quest was at an end – she'd helped free Igor, and win Boris back his father's throne. She should feel victorious, happy, triumphant…but all she felt was emptiness inside.

"Shall we go home, Father?" she asked.

Father shook his head. "No, we'll be expected to sit at the high table for the feast. Bela likes to pretend I am his pet assassin, to frighten any enemies he might have, and I lost a wager today, so I must pay him what is owed. You…should enjoy the feast. There will be food and wine and dancing, and more courtiers than you can count, at least after you've had a few cups of wine. Perhaps one of them might catch your eye, or it may be that you develop a taste for court life, and that you'd like a place here. Tonight will be your victory feast, and you should celebrate." He guided her out of the chamber, then waved for a servant. "Can you show us where we shall sleep tonight?" he asked.

The flustered maid dropped a deep curtsy as she stammered out, "I…do not know, my lord. I shall find out directly." She hurried away.

"Oh, and your fairy godmother will return at midnight, after she's dealt with the shoes girl, or whatever it was. In case you need help with anything," Father said.

Forty-Five

Boris had attended many feasts, even sitting at the king's right hand, but he suspected this was the one he would least remember, for he had eyes only for Rossa in her red gown. He'd never thought he'd want another woman in his life after Vica, but now…he wanted nothing else. And he'd give up the throne and all the honours Bela wanted to heap on him, if only Rossa would smile at him again.

Of course, he could scarcely see her while they both sat at opposite ends of the high table, and he'd lost count of the number of courtiers who'd come up to talk to him, hoping to earn a place in his favour early on. Much might have changed in two centuries, but the self-interest of the king's courtiers was ever constant.

Boris drank sparingly, waiting for the feast to end so he might seek out Rossa to speak with her. But King Bela had other ideas, commanding the musicians to play something they might dance to. Boris quickly realised he would only embarrass himself in attempting to join the complicated dances, for that much had changed since he'd last been at court. He glanced at Rossa, wondering if she knew these modern dances. Perhaps he could persuade her to teach him…

But her place was empty, as was her father's. Boris scanned the room, searching every face for the one he wanted most. It was her gown that caught his eye, a quick flash of red before she vanished through a side door.

Boris excused himself and followed.

The door led to a dark passage, then another, until he glimpsed light around the corner. He crept closer.

"I must apologise for my lateness. I promised I would stay at the ball until midnight, if she needed my help, but she did not. I waited until the very last moment, too. I hope she and her prince will be very happy. Even if she did lose her shoes..." he heard Zuleika say.

"Do your god-daughters usually marry princes? Are you supposed to act as matchmaker?" Rossa asked.

Zuleika sighed. "I'm supposed to help them when they have no other hope of happiness. Sometimes with little warning, too, so that I am forced to portal thousands of miles in a night in order to be in two places at once. I don't know how my mother managed it all, to be honest. But I infinitely prefer it to staying tied to one court, so there is that."

"I wish I could travel. This is the first time Father has let me leave Mother's lands, but the more I see, the more I want to know. Like whether all courts are like this one, or if everyone eats the same dishes, or does the same dances, or even plays the same music. Or what the ocean tastes like. Or how desert sands would feel beneath my feet. Or…"

Zuleika laughed. "Sounds like you should do my job for a while, if only to see some of the world. Heaven knows I could do with the help. Ah, but then there is your prince to think about…"

"Boris is not my prince." Rossa's voice sounded so flat.

"That's not what it looked like when I arrived at your home. Unless you've had a disagreement…in which case, perhaps I can help?"

Rossa sighed. "No, there is no disagreement between us. I agreed to help him win back his father's throne. The king has named him his heir before all the court – he has his heart's desire. He no longer needs me, so I should go home. Yet I have this yearning not to…"

"You wish to stay here, then?"

"No! I want to see the world. One court is not enough."

"A pity, for your prince will be king one day, and he will need a queen, for that's how succession usually works."

"Could you see me as a queen?"

"Well, you certainly have the bearing for it. Not to mention the right gown and jewels to impress even this court. You'd need to wear a crown, though…what of this one?"

"Don't be silly!"

"I see nothing silly about it. It's quite stately, in my opinion."

Boris edged closer, hoping to catch a glimpse of Rossa in a crown, if her godmother succeeded in persuading her.

"Here, let me help you," Zuleika said, turning Rossa to face her. She lifted his mother's ruby and diamond crown high into the air and took several tries to settle it among Rossa's dark curls.

Boris swore he saw Zuleika wink at him before turning her attention back to Rossa.

"Now, Crown Princess Rossa, nay, Queen Rossa, for that's who would wear such a crown, you must sit on the throne," Zuleika said.

"That's going too far. What if someone sees us?"

"Then you should do it quickly, for what other opportunity will you have to know what it feels like to be a crowned queen, seated upon your throne?"

Fearless Rossa did not hesitate. She ascended the dais, and took her rightful place upon the throne, staring out across the throne room as if it were filled with courtiers and not shadows.

Boris's mouth went dry. He would dream of this sight. Of Rossa in all her glory. And wish…

"It suits you," Zuleika said.

"No, I…"

Boris stepped forward. "It does. That is indeed the queen's crown, which was only worn a few times a year, at the most important events. Bela promised you a crown, and I think you should tell him you want that one."

Rossa shuddered and set the crown aside. "King Bela is an old man. He might be a wise and just king, but I could never marry him."

Boris's heart sank. "And I am so much older than him. If I were to ask…would you refuse me, too?" He had to know.

"I…"

Boris closed his eyes. He wanted to become

the bear again, a creature who did not mourn or cry, but who might run forever.

Rossa swallowed. "I'm not ready to marry yet. I've seen so little of the world, and I want to see so much more. If my father would only allow me…"

"You are an adult, are you not? Mistress of your own fate? Your father cannot control you forever. Your fate is your own, and he has no choice in the matter."

Zuleika dropped a silent curtsy, cast a spell that unleashed a blinding light, and when Boris managed to blink the bright blindness from his eyes, she had gone.

Rossa managed a smile. "Even my fairy godmother is afraid of my father. No one dares risk his ire, for his reputation precedes him."

Boris took her hands. "I'm not afraid of him. If you wish to travel the world, come with me. King Bela has named me Captain of the Varangian Guard, just as my father did, for the Emperor has dismissed them and sent them home. We will defend the borders, and protect our own people, going wherever we are needed. I've seen you fight. We would be honoured to have you with us, as you earn a name for yourself, separate from your father's."

"Truly?"

"Truly."

Rossa threw her arms around his neck and kissed him. What started as a chaste peck did not stay so for long. Boris drank deeply, as though her breath were wine, wishing he could never let her go. Like that night in the cave, when he'd first regained his manly form, thanks to her.

Her thoughts seemed to mirror his own. "Take me to bed, Snow."

"Are you sure, my Rose? I haven't asked you to marry me yet, let alone said the vows."

She met his gaze, unflinching. "One day, when the time is right, you will ask. And on that day, I will say yes."

"And one day, you will sit on that throne beside me, with the queen's crown on your head."

"Yes."

"Can I persuade you to wear it to bed? Just

the crown and nothing else?"

Rossa laughed. "Perhaps."

He set the crown upon her head, then swept her up in his arms. "My bedchamber, or yours?"

"Whichever one has the bigger bed."

Down the in the great hall, the festivities went on, while Rossa and Boris barred the door of his bedchamber. Court clothes slid to the floor, no longer necessary for two people who only wanted each other. Maiden she might be, but Rossa was as ready for Boris as he was for her, and she did not hesitate. A blissful gasp was the only sound she made as their bodies became one, and Boris swore nothing and no one would ever part them again.

About the Author

Demelza Carlton has always loved the ocean, but on her first snorkelling trip she found she was afraid of fish.

She has since swum with sea lions, sharks and sea cucumbers and stood on spray drenched cliffs over a seething sea as a seven-metre cyclonic swell surged in, shattering a shipwreck below.

Demelza now lives in Perth, Western Australia, the shark attack capital of the world.

The *Ocean's Gift* series was her first foray into fiction, followed by her suspense thriller *Nightmares* trilogy. She swears the *Mel Goes to Hell* series ambushed her on a crowded train and wouldn't leave her alone.

Want to know more? You can follow Demelza on Facebook, Twitter, YouTube or her website, Demelza Carlton's Place at:

www.demelzacarlton.com

More Books by Demelza Carlton

<u>Colony: Holiday series</u>

Cowboys and Aliens (#1)

Ghost (#2)

Vulcan (#3)

Cupid (#4)

Valentine(#5)

Prometheus (#6)

<u>**Colony: Aqua series**</u>

Halcyon (#1)

Poseidon (#2)

Apollo (#3)

<u>**Colony: Nyx series**</u>

Fang (#1)

Talon (#2)

Claw (#3)

<u>**Siren of War series**</u>

Ocean's Justice (#1)

Ocean's Widow (#2)

Ocean's Bride (#3)

Ocean's Rise (#4)

Ocean's War (#5)

How To Catch Crabs

<u>**Nightmares Trilogy**</u>

Nightmares of Caitlin Lockyer (#1)

Necessary Evil of Nathan Miller (#2)

Afterlife of Alana Miller (#3)

<u>**Romance Island Resort series**</u>
Maid for the Rock Star (#1)
The Rock Star's Email Order Bride (#2)
The Rock Star's Virginity (#3)
The Rock Star and the Billionaire (#4)
The Rock Star Wants A Wife (#5)
The Rock Star's Wedding (#6)
Maid for the South Pole (#7)

<u>Romance a Medieval Fairytale series</u>

Enchant: Beauty and the Beast Retold

Dance: Cinderella Retold

Fly: Goose Girl Retold

Revel: Twelve Dancing Princesses
Retold

Silence: Little Mermaid Retold

Awaken: Sleeping Beauty Retold

Embellish: Brave Little Tailor Retold

Appease: Princess and the Pea Retold

Blow: Three Little Pigs Retold

Return: Hansel and Gretel Retold

Wish: Aladdin Retold

Melt: Snow Queen Retold

Spin: Rumpelstiltskin Retold

Kiss: Frog Prince Retold

Reflect: Snow White Retold

Roar: Goldilocks Retold

Cobble: Elves and the Shoemaker Retold

Float: Enchanted Horse Retold

Steal: Forty Thieves Retold

Call: Pied Piper Retold

Fall: Scheherazade Retold

Feather: Swan Maidens Retold

Cross: Billy Goats Gruff Retold

Weave: Rapunzel Retold

Claim: Puss in Boots Retold

Curse: Rose Red Retold

Cross: Three Billy Goats Gruff Retold

Weave: Rapunzel Retold

Claim: Puss in Boots Retold

<u>**Heart of Stone series**</u>

Heart of Steel (#0)

Broken Chains (#1)

Broken Bonds (#2)

Broken Dreams (#3)

<u>**Heart of Steel series**</u>

Heart of Steel (#0)

Stone Guardian (#1)

Stone Champion (#2)

Stone Sentinel (#3)

Stone Shadow (#4)

9 781925 799491